Totally Five Star: Madrid

THE KING OF INFIERNO

JASMINE HILL

The King of Infierno
ISBN # 978-1-78430-659-5
©Copyright Jasmine Hill 2015
Cover Art by Posh Gosh ©Copyright June 2015
Interior text design by Claire Siemaszkiewicz
Totally Bound Publishing

Published in 2015 by Totally Bound Publishing, Newland House, The Point, Weaver Road, Lincoln, LN6 3QN, United Kingdom.

Totally Bound Publishing is a subsidiary of Totally Entwined Group Limited.

THE KING OF INFIERNO

Dedication

To my husband.

Chapter One

Donovan King had never before laid eyes on such a beautiful creature. She looked like an angel. Her golden hair tumbled in careless waves past her shoulders. Her plump, cherry red lips looked lush and full. But it was her eyes that mesmerized him. Even behind those thick, black-rimmed glasses, her eyes were the first feature he noticed. A color that he'd heard about but had never actually seen on someone in the flesh—violet eyes. There were purple smudges under them, the only thing marring her lovely features, indicating a weariness that someone so young should never have to endure.

A threadbare, baggy jumper and a long floral skirt hid most of her figure, but he could tell, even under her shapeless clothing, that she was slender, too slender. Her wrist that poked out of one floppy sleeve was so pale and delicate that he imagined the simplest flick of his fingers could snap it in two—the thought sent a cold jolt through him.

He peered out of the window of the service station and studied the cars, his gaze alighting on a beat-up old Commodore that had definitely seen better days. He'd bet his left arm that the car was hers. Anger suffused him. How could anyone allow this young woman to drive such a deathtrap? Didn't she have anyone looking out for her interests? He shuddered to think what could happen to her if she ever broke down alone and at night.

Donovan snapped his gaze back to the woman, her increasingly frantic movements drawing his attention once more. She looked panicked and had ducked her head to rummage through a shabby handbag.

He looked past her to the service station attendant who kept drumming his fingers impatiently. Donovan lowered his gaze to a crumpled five-dollar note and a few coins scattered on the counter.

The angel looked up, her face flushed, hands shaking. "I know I have it. Just a moment."

Her sexy voice, husky and low, hit him like a sledgehammer. It was deeper than he'd expected and sent hot desire unfurling in his belly.

A gruff cough from farther back in the growing line spurred Donovan into action. One long stride brought him level with the counter. "How much?" he snarled at the attendant.

"Ten bucks."

Donovan threw a ten-dollar note onto the counter and scooped up the money the woman had already deposited there. He grasped one of her delicate hands in his and tugged her gently away from the other customers.

He realized just how petite she was when he drew her close. She stared up at him, her violet eyes wide behind those ugly glasses. The flush on her cheeks intensified as she visibly struggled to regain her composure.

"I'm so sorry, sir," she murmured in that husky voice.

Fuck! Did she just call me sir? His testosterone levels flew into hyperdrive.

"I know I have the money in here somewhere." She opened her handbag and recommenced rummaging through it.

Donovan placed a hand on her arm, stilling her frantic movements.

"Don't apologize. Please, I was happy to help." He thrust the money he'd reclaimed from the attendant into her hand.

"Oh, thank you, but I can't possibly accept," she said.

"You can and you will," he stated bluntly. "No arguments."

She gazed at him, indecision clouding her beautiful eyes. She grasped the hem of her jumper and twisted the fabric between her hands as she nibbled on her bottom lip. She was younger than he'd first thought, definitely early twenties, and her whole doe-eyed, breathy-voiced demeanor was sending his protective instincts into overdrive. The power of the unfamiliar emotion was so strong he had to force himself to refrain from picking her up and striding to his car with her safely in his arms. He shoved a hand through his hair in agitation.

She seemed to come to a decision and thrust a hand out in his direction. "My name's Makayla Carrington. Thank you, sir, for helping me. It was very kind of you."

Fierce desire swept through him. *There's that word again.* He struggled to maintain his composure as he took her hand in his and lifted it to his lips. "Makayla,

I'm Donovan King. It's a pleasure to make your acquaintance."

A frisson like an electric shot hit him when he touched her. It was an odd thing for him to do, kiss a woman's hand. He couldn't remember ever having done it before. He was definitely not a man given to romantic gestures. His proclivities ran deeper and darker than that.

She blushed prettily, lowered her eyes and grasped her bag to her chest in a defensive gesture. "Well, I need to go. Thank you again for your kindness."

Panic overtook him at the thought that he might never see her again. But before he could think of something to keep her from leaving, she'd turned and was walking toward the door. He followed and made his way to his Lexus, sliding into the car quickly, his intention of purchasing a bottle of water suddenly forgotten. He watched as she strode to the beat-up old Commodore and slipped into the driver's seat.

She hadn't looked around, hadn't appeared remotely curious about him, but seemed to have forgotten his existence almost the moment he was out of her sight. The thought that she could be so unaffected by him was infuriating.

He studied his drab surroundings and questioned how he'd found himself in such a part of Sydney. He was glad that he'd stopped, however, if for no other reason than encountering the captivating creature named Makayla.

He didn't even think about what he was doing—he was operating on autopilot, the need to see her again was his only concern.

He sat quietly and waited for her to start her car. She fiddled around and looked to be checking her mobile phone. Finally, she started the ignition and pulled out of the service station.

Donovan started his engine and followed behind her. His car's windows were tinted and as it was dusk, he had no concerns that she would see him. And, after all, she hadn't even been curious enough to look around for him or his car. He had no other choice, he had to follow her — it was his only hope of finding her again.

Chapter Two

Makayla was distracted and tired. Beyond tired, in fact, and hitting the realms of exhaustion. She'd had a busy few days and was relieved to have finally delivered her last basket of mending to its owner. Her mother's mental state hadn't helped. Josephine had had a bad week and had required almost constant supervision. That, added to the mending that Makayla took on to augment their meager income, meant that she'd managed little sleep. She huffed in frustration. Obviously, her mother's new meds weren't working, and she'd have to make another doctor's appointment.

Her mind wandered to Donovan King, the gentleman at the service station. Initially, she'd been struck dumb by his appearance. He was extremely handsome and tall. She guessed at least six foot two, so he towered over her petite, four-foot-five frame. He'd been dressed in a bespoke suit, the fabric so fine that she'd found herself wanting to reach out and stroke it. His dark hair fell in unruly waves to just below his ears and his cinnamon-colored eyes seemed to bore right through her. He had a hard jaw, described as chiseled in the books she read. His movie star good looks had been enough to make her tongue-tied, but he also had an intimidating presence, which was enhanced by his powerful physique. It had taken her a moment to gather her composure and an odd butterfly effect had settled in her belly.

She knew she'd never see him again and the thought saddened her. Odd, as she'd just met him and the meeting was only an exchange of names, nothing concrete. But something about him had stirred feelings deep inside her. Of course, she'd more than appreciated his paying for her fuel. That episode had been embarrassing to say the least. There was nothing more mortifying than being caught short of funds — particularly as she could hardly siphon the fuel back out of her tank. But it was more than his kindness to her. She'd felt an irresistible pull toward him, an intense attraction that she hadn't ever felt before. She'd been so tied in knots that she hadn't even thought to ask for his number so she could do something to return his kindness — that would have been a perfect excuse to see him again. But then, why would such an obviously successful and handsome man be interested in her? She was plain and awkward and definitely not a woman in the league of someone so sophisticated and sure of himself. She was his polar opposite — inexperienced, ordinary and gawky. She had few friends, no social life and hadn't ever even had a boyfriend. It wasn't because she didn't *want* those things. It was just her way of life. For as long as she could remember, she'd been caring for her mother. She'd only managed to go to school because their neighbor, Mrs. Young, would stay with Josephine during the day. In return, Makayla would cook and clean for the elderly lady. It was an arrangement that had suited them all for a time.

Then Josephine's behavior had started to become more erratic, to the point where Makayla had only been one month into her diploma in fashion design and textiles before she'd had to withdraw from the course. When she'd received five frantic phone calls from Mrs. Young in one week, it had been glaringly obvious that she'd be unable to continue with her studies. Instead, she stayed home with her mother and took on sewing and mending work to supplement her mother's disability pension and her small caregiver's allowance. She'd only managed to get her driver's license because the retired schoolteacher across the road had taught her to drive in exchange for casseroles and cakes. She was grateful for the goodwill of her neighbors, which meant that she'd been able to keep her mother at home, and it had kept Makayla out of the foster care system.

Her mother's mental instability had been growing worse and her doctor was becoming increasingly concerned, reiterating that he was only treating the symptoms but not the cause, and that her mother's mental state needed to be analyzed by specialists. He was now talking about a long-term care facility to provide intensive therapy. That had sounded like a solution until Makayla had visited some of the state-run institutions and decided there and then that there was no way she could commit her mother to such a place. While there was nothing outwardly wrong with them, it was painfully obvious that they were underfunded and understaffed and she doubted that her mother would receive the intensive care and therapy that she required. No, as far as Makayla was concerned, the current situation was the best that they could hope for. She managed each day by not thinking of the future. She enjoyed cooking and sewing and found solace in those relaxing activities.

She couldn't go out at night and leave her mother alone, so she'd never attended a party. Her few friends from school had virtually drifted away and stopped asking her to movies and clubs. Makayla supposed that she could have managed a night out here and there, but if she was honest with herself, she didn't go for fear of having *too much* fun. She was scared that if she got a taste of the social life, a taste of everything she'd been missing, then she'd be unhappy and resentful of her current state of affairs. So she stayed at home.

Her one vice was the erotic romance novels she read at night. Only then could she allow herself to dream. Tucked up in bed, knowing her mother was safely installed in the next room, meant that Makayla could relax and immerse herself in the stories of love and romance. She lived vicariously through the heroes and heroines, experienced love and turmoil, sex and heartache via the pages of her books. At the age of twenty-two, she was still, embarrassingly, very much a virgin. If she'd had the energy and the appropriate outgoing personality, she would have rectified the situation before now. But as she was not the type to instigate or enjoy a one-night stand, and her chance of meeting a man and entering into a relationship seemed hopeless, she supposed that she'd live with the condition indefinitely. She'd experienced her fair share of making out and heavy petting with a boy from school, but when she'd found herself ready to take the next sexual step, she hadn't been in a personal situation to do so. Her erotic novels and some heavy petting of her own managed to satisfy, albeit mildly unsatisfactorily, any sexual urges that she had.

She pulled up outside the modest home she shared with her mother. Her internal monolog and musings seeming to have switched another part of her brain into autopilot, and she couldn't remember the drive home from the service station.

She gathered her handbag and belongings and made her way up to the house. Lights glowed and the television flickered behind the closed curtains of the lounge, all of which gave her a warm, comforting feeling. It meant that everything inside was as it should be.

Makayla let herself into the house and found Mrs. Young knitting and watching a soap opera on TV. Her mother sat in a dressing gown, asleep in an armchair.

"Hello, dear," Grace Young greeted her cheerfully. "Josephine has had a shower and a sandwich for dinner. I had to give her a mild sedative. She started to become rather anxious, talking about your father and plans for the weekend. I couldn't get her to settle down and I was worried that she was preparing for a disappearing act."

Makayla frowned. "Thank you, Grace. She's been on about Dad quite a bit lately. Why don't we leave Mum here to doze and you come join me in the kitchen while I put something together for dinner."

Makayla settled Mrs. Young at the table with a cup of tea then puttered around the kitchen, only half listening to her neighbor chatting about what had happened at her weekly bingo night. She enjoyed these times when she felt relaxed and at peace. She liked listening to Mrs. Young's idle gossip as she prepared their evening meal and even laughed at her neighbor's unwarranted cooking advice.

The truth was that both she and Mrs. Young enjoyed each other's company. Makayla for a brief respite, hearing mindless dialog, and Grace for being the provider of said dialog. Makayla valued the times when her mother could join them for dinner. However, in her down days, Josephine didn't eat a great deal and was anything but social. Makayla and Mrs. Young avoided sedating her when possible, except Josephine's increasing instability was worrying, and Makayla had instructed Grace to give her a mild sedative if she was concerned about her mother's intentions. She abhorred medicating her in such a way, but she couldn't see an alternative. Her mother was beautiful, fun-loving and gregarious. Lately, though, nothing seemed to settle her or calm her. Mrs. Young was too old to gallivant about the countryside in search of Makayla if Mum did a disappearing act, so for the moment, they were left with few alternatives.

She shook off her feeling of melancholy and prepared a light meal of marinated grilled chicken and vegetables, which Mrs. Young tucked into with gusto. Makayla's appetite was not as hearty and she only picked at her meal, her mind returning again and again to Donovan King. She also worried about her mother and she determined to make a doctor's appointment first thing Monday morning. She wasn't relishing the visit, however, as she knew that he would once again start in on her mother needing intensive therapy. Makayla couldn't seem to get across to him that it was impossible — at least impossible to get her *decent* and *worthwhile* care — without sufficient funds. Her only savior was the fact that her mother had not proven to be a danger to anyone, herself excluded. Her ups consisted of her doing ridiculous, personally reckless things, like the time she'd disappeared for four days. Makayla had eventually found her in a hotel in the next state, looking disheveled and exhausted after having spent her time partying at the local bars. In her down days, it was an effort for Makayla even to get her out of bed. Makayla prayed that the doctor could find something to stabilize her mum's moods and that at the very least her mother could start leading a semi-normal life.

She sighed in weariness. It was only seven on Friday evening and she felt like she could sleep for a week. Tomorrow was another day, she told herself. Perhaps there was light at the end of the tunnel.

She had one more thing that she wanted to do before she finally fell into bed—Google Donovan King.

Chapter Three

Makayla awoke slowly, her brain still sleep addled. She'd stayed up later than usual checking the Internet for Donovan King and had been surprised when Google had displayed hundreds of hits. According to the accounts, he was thirty-one and the owner of numerous nightclubs across Sydney. He attended various social and charity events and always had a beautiful woman hanging off his arm. She learned two things—he looked fantastic in a tuxedo and he seemed to have a bevy of beauties to choose from when he required a date. He was rarely seen with the same woman more than twice. Makayla wasn't surprised. She knew just by his good looks and obvious sophistication that he wouldn't ever be in want of female company. *Was there someone particularly special to him?* She wasn't even sure why she'd bothered to appease her curiosity as it had just left her feeling depressed.

She stretched and checked her bedside clock—eight-thirty. *Shit.* Her mother had only taken a mild sedative, which meant that she would have been awake and alert in the early hours.

She jumped out of bed and raced next door to Josephine's room, knocking once before barging in unannounced.

Her mother was sitting up in bed watching a morning talk show. "Hi, sweetie. What's the emergency?"

Makayla almost withered on the spot in relief. "Hi, Mum. I was just checking to see if you were okay."

Her mother opened her arms for a hug, and Makayla ran to her, enveloping her in a tight embrace. She stayed there for a moment, unwilling to let go. Her mother's good times were becoming few and far between, and when she had them, Makayla wanted every moment to last.

"How are you feeling this morning, Mum?" Makayla gazed up at her. "You're looking well."

Her mother frowned. "I can't recall going to bed last night."

Makayla sat up and smiled. "That's because Grace slipped you a Mickey."

They looked at each other a moment then burst into peals of laughter.

"Oh, Makayla, was I that bad?" she asked, wiping tears of mirth from her eyes.

"No, Mum. Grace was just a little concerned. I was delivering the mending to my customers and she was worried that you were…in one of your moods."

Her mothered sobered instantly. "Makayla, I've told you time and again that this isn't healthy for you, or for me, for that matter. You're young and you need to be out socializing. You need to be *living* your life, not stuck here day after day, looking after me."

"Mum, let's not ruin a good day by rehashing things."

Her mother sighed. "Okay, but I want you to promise me that you'll start looking out for *you*,

Makayla. I know what my problems are doing to your life and it's not fair."

"I'll make another appointment with Dr. Fraser. Hopefully a change in your meds will help stabilize your moods."

Her mother gave her a sad smile. "We can only hope."

* * * *

Donovan felt like a stalker. He'd been sitting outside Makayla's house for two hours. He hadn't worked out exactly what he was going to do if he did see her. He'd play that by ear. Acting like a lovesick puppy was so far outside his usual behavior as to be startling. He never chased women — he didn't need to. Women had a propensity to throw themselves at him and he had an inclination to take advantage of that. Now here he was pursuing a woman, but he couldn't seem to help himself. There was something about her that drew him and he knew he wouldn't rest until he got closer to her. He recalled the frisson of electricity that had zapped through him when he'd touched her. Something, until it had happened to him, that he'd always dismissed as fancy. He'd also surreptitiously checked for any ring to indicate if she was taken. She hadn't been wearing anything, but he knew that didn't account for much. Still, she was young, too young to be married, at least in his estimation. He had to hope that there was no boyfriend on the scene.

As if in answer to his thoughts, the front door opened and she stepped out. His heart skipped a beat at the sight of her. Dressed in a long floral skirt and cardigan, she looked beautiful and fresh. She had piled her hair on top of her head, wavy tendrils framing her face. She wasn't wearing those ugly black glasses and the difference to her face was striking. She strode down the path to the letterbox.

It's now or never.

Donovan opened his car door and stepped out. She looked up at the sound and stopped dead, a frown crossing her features. He walked toward her slowly, not wanting to alarm her and more than aware that his appearance on her doorstep would look odd enough.

He smiled as he drew nearer. "Hi." He shoved his hands in his pockets, hoping to affect a casual stance.

"Hello." She drew the word out in obvious confusion.

"I know how this looks," he started to explain. "I don't usually follow women home. In fact, this is the first time." He laughed. "But I had to see you again. Can I take you out for dinner?"

Chapter Four

Makayla was dumbfounded. This godlike creature had actually followed her home and was now asking her out? She couldn't help but be a little suspicious. What could he possibly want from her? She was hardly in the league of women he was usually seen out with. She wasn't tall or sophisticated and she wasn't particularly curvy. She was too slender. She eyed him doubtfully for a moment as she tried to formulate an answer to his question.

He grinned. "You don't know me, of course. But I promise you that I'm not a deranged serial killer." He handed her a business card.

Curiously, it wasn't what Makayla had been thinking. He didn't frighten her, even turning up as he had, but exactly the opposite—she was drawn to him. No, her suspicions were founded on something entirely different. She made a snap decision. What could it hurt to talk to him at least? She desperately needed a distraction. However, she didn't think she'd be able to manage an evening out. Her mother's state was too delicate.

"Actually, I am in your debt for helping me yesterday. Why don't you come to dinner at my house tonight? I'll cook for you. It's…difficult for me to get out in the evenings. My mother isn't well." She hoped she sounded more confident than she felt. There was something about the man that rattled her. It was more than his impossibly good looks and rock-hard body—at least she was willing to bet he had a rock-hard body. It was an intensity he had about him when he looked at her, which gave her goosebumps and sent shivers rippling down her spine.

She looked up at him from beneath lowered lashes. Would he accept her offer or would he see it as too unattractive an activity? Particularly with the assumption that her mother would be included in the dinner. She was just about to withdraw the invitation as silly and thoughtless when he spoke up.

"I'd love to join you for dinner. I'll bring the wine. What time should I arrive?"

"Does seven-thirty work for you?"

"Seven-thirty is perfect," he murmured, reaching out and running a finger down her cheek.

Makayla gasped as, once again, little currents of energy shot to her core. It was uncanny and more than a little unnerving.

"You feel it too," he said softly. "I needed to touch you again to ensure I hadn't imagined it. Until tonight, sweet Makayla."

* * * *

Makayla's stomach was tied in knots. She wanted everything to be perfect. She'd only suggested that evening for dinner because Josephine was having a good day, which meant that at least she'd be talkative and enjoy the company. It didn't mean that her mother wouldn't have a meltdown halfway through dinner, but Makayla had decided to risk it. It was another reason for her nervousness and she'd asked herself numerous times whether it had been a terrible idea to invite Donovan into their home.

She'd raced out just after Donovan had left, to buy supplies. She'd forgotten to ask him if there was anything he didn't or couldn't eat. Sending a text to him at the number on his business card would have been easy enough, but she didn't want to bother him. She eventually decided on steak, asparagus and new potatoes served with a Béarnaise sauce. Her instincts told her that he would be very much a meat eater. For dessert, she'd made a strawberry mousse. Makayla pulled out their best dinnerware, which rarely saw the light of day and had originally belonged to her grandmother, and spread a white damask tablecloth on the dining room table to hide its scratched surface. It had never bothered her before, but then they rarely entertained, their main visitor being Mrs. Young from next door.

Her mother was like a tin of worms, demanding to know how she'd met Donovan and pushing her for information about him. Makayla could only repeat what she'd learned on the Internet and explain how he'd rescued her from certain mortification by paying for her fuel. Josephine commented that he must be a true gentleman to have saved a damsel in distress. Makayla thought that that was taking things a little too far, but she enjoyed her mother's enthusiasm.

Her biggest decision, other than what to cook, was what to wear. Her wardrobe didn't include many sophisticated choices. She loved fashion and it was what she'd planned on for a career—designing and textiles. She just hadn't had the time to dedicate to her own wardrobe.

Makayla eventually decided on a pair of dark jeans and a soft, woolen, indigo-colored jumper that Mrs. Young had knitted her for her birthday. The color brought out the violet in her eyes and she always felt pretty wearing it. She fixed her heavy length of hair into a messy topknot and kept her makeup to a dusting of powder, mascara, lip gloss and a spritz of perfume. The trick was to look like she'd made an effort but not to go too overboard. It was just dinner at home, after all.

Makayla surveyed herself in the mirror and was happy with the result. She felt pretty and feminine, which boosted her self-confidence. The only problem was her glasses. They were not the most attractive pair she'd ever owned. In fact, they were a spare pair. Her other glasses had a crack through one lens. She decided quickly to do without them. They were only for reading and the fine sewing work she had to do, but she was just so used to hiding behind them that she felt a little exposed without them.

As she was leaving her room, the doorbell rang. She opened the door to find Donovan leaning against the jamb, holding a large bunch of colorful flowers and some wine. Her heart skipped a beat at the sight of him. His brown hair, still damp from a shower, curled to just below his ears. His white open-necked shirt, rolled up at the sleeves, revealed tanned, muscular forearms, and his faded jeans hung off his hips deliciously. His lightly stubbled jaw gave him a rakish edge, immediately bringing sand and sunsets to mind. He was everything male wrapped up into one very appealing package.

He smirked and cocked an eyebrow. "Are you going to invite me in?"

Makayla flushed. What was she thinking, standing and staring at him like a star-struck fool? "Of course, I'm sorry." She moved aside and motioned him through the door.

He stopped on the threshold. "You look beautiful," he murmured appreciatively. "That color really brings out your eyes." He handed her the bunch of flowers and a box of chocolates that she hadn't noticed him holding. "The flowers are for you and the chocolates are for your mother." He winked. "I have to sweeten her up."

Makayla virtually expired on the spot. Could he have been any more charming?

Her mother appeared at her side. "You must be Donovan. It's so nice to meet you." She held out her hand in greeting.

Donovan took her hand in his. "The pleasure is all mine, Mrs. Carrington."

Josephine tittered. It was amusing to see her so taken aback. It wasn't just Makayla who found herself overwhelmed in Donovan's presence. It was good to see that even her mother wasn't immune to his good looks and charm.

"Please, call me Josephine," she finally told him.

He held up two bottles of wine. "I brought white and red. I wasn't sure what was on the menu."

"I hope you like steak," Makayla said as she took the bottles of wine from him and led them into the lounge.

He gave her a winning smile. "Steak is one of my favorites."

Chapter Five

When Makayla had opened the door, Donovan had done a double take. Her eyes sparkled and her lips, glossed in pink, were lush and full. He wanted to kiss her. And that hair, so copious and tied into a mess on top of her head, made him think of sex and beds — thoughts he'd had to curb quickly for fear of embarrassing himself.

He'd enjoyed dinner immensely. It was clear that Makayla was a fabulous cook. The steak was grilled to perfection and served with the best Béarnaise sauce he'd ever tasted, followed by a delicious strawberry mousse that had melted in his mouth.

Her mother had been welcoming too, but quiet, and after dessert she'd retired to her bedroom, mentioning something about her medication making her drowsy.

Now he was sitting in the lounge next to Makayla, drinking coffee. "Thank you for a lovely meal. You're a wonderful cook."

She blushed. "It was nothing. Quite simple, really."

"You must learn how to take a compliment, Makayla."

She fidgeted and gazed into her lap. "Well, it was nice to have some company and to thank you for helping me."

Donovan studied her over the rim of his coffee mug. She really was intriguing. She seemed so innocent yet projected a maturity beyond her years. He'd discovered over dinner that she was only twenty-two. She was younger than the women he usually dated. Well, women he went out with on occasion. He didn't date as a rule, and was ashamed to admit that he most often sought his partners for activities that didn't include a lot of deep and meaningful conversation. He'd had two long-term relationships, neither of which had ended amicably. But here was this beautiful, sweet angel who'd stumbled into his path and turned him inside out in a matter of moments. She was too good for him, too pure, even a little naïve. It was the way she looked at him—full of wide-eyed vulnerability. He suspected that she wasn't very experienced and he sensed that he'd need to move slowly with her. She didn't look like the type of girl to leap straight into bed with a guy she'd just met, and the thought pleased him.

Finally, she looked up at him and smiled. "I have to confess, I've Googled you," she announced. "I'm sorry if that seems like an invasion of your privacy, but I wanted to know more about you."

"I'm glad you did," he conceded. "After all, you invited me into your home. I like that you had the forethought to do some investigation of me. At the very least, you know I am who I say I am."

She looked suddenly uncomfortable. "Do you have a girlfriend? I know it's none of my business. I'm just asking because I've seen a lot of photos of you with beautiful women."

Of course, she'd seen the copious images of him with various women. Christ knew what she thought of him. Even to his eyes, he looked like a man whore. "No, I don't have a girlfriend. I wouldn't be here having dinner with you if I did."

She looked relieved and it gave him a glimmer of hope that she, perhaps, felt some attraction toward him. Up until this point, it had been hard to tell. She kept her emotions close. She was polite and talkative, but she hadn't been overtly friendly, hadn't even embarked on a little harmless flirting. It wasn't what he was used to, and he found himself floundering to the point where he was pathetically grateful for any scraps of attention she threw his way. He knew she felt the physical attraction as he did — the sparks of electricity that had zapped between them when they'd touched. She'd gasped when he'd stroked her cheek that morning. So why did he feel that he had to work so hard to gain her affection? She stifled a yawn, and he suddenly realized how tired she looked. The smudges under her eyes weren't as dark as they had been the previous day, but they were still there — the only blemishes in an otherwise beautiful face. He should go and leave her to go to bed.

He looked at his watch. "It's getting late. Thank you, once again, for a lovely meal."

She looked panicked. He smiled inwardly — finally, a positive reaction from her. It gave him the confidence he needed to make his next move.

"I'll pick you up tomorrow at seven-thirty. We'll go to dinner." He worded it as a statement deliberately. He didn't want to give her an option. He needed her to realize that he *would* take her out. And besides, it was who he was. He liked to be in control at all times, and it was better that she realized that about his nature sooner rather than later.

Her eyes widened in surprise, then she frowned, catching her bottom lip between her teeth. "I can't," she finally murmured. "But thank you for the invitation."

What the fuck? He was taken aback, he couldn't recall any woman refusing an invitation from him. Then again, he hadn't actually *invited* Makayla, but rather had *told* her. Perhaps it was his method of delivery that she objected to.

He leaned forward in his chair, elbows on his knees, hands clasped. "I'm sorry if I sounded abrupt. When I want something, I go after it."

"It's not that." She smiled. "Though your way of asking me out was...unique. It's that I don't like to leave my mother alone for too long. Mrs. Young, our neighbor, comes over during the day if I have to go out, but I don't like to ask her to help during her evenings too."

Donovan frowned. Josephine had seemed okay to him during dinner. Admittedly, she had been a little quiet, but he hadn't noticed anything physically wrong with her. Then again, he was no doctor. What was so bad that she couldn't be left alone? As if in answer to his musings, Makayla started to explain.

"My mother has bipolar disorder, and the doctor thinks mild schizophrenia too. She has her good days and bad days. Today was a good day, but we can never be sure when her mood is going to change. Nine times out of ten, I could go out and everything would be fine. The problem is—I can't be sure. When she has a manic episode, she becomes very unstable and unpredictable. It used to be that we could recognize the onset of a manic occurrence, but in the last few years her condition has worsened and her moods change quite quickly. We're trying her on different meds but it's…complicated."

That explains why Makayla looks so tired. She's worried about her mother.

"I'm sorry," he said softly. "It must be very difficult for you."

She gave him a weak smile. "We get by. We have each other, and Mrs. Young is very good to us."

He took one of her hands in his. "I had a lovely evening, Makayla. I'll let you go to bed. You need your sleep."

He stood swiftly and walked to the front door, pausing by it. Makayla followed and opened it for him, standing uncertainly on the threshold. It was all he could do to stop himself from grasping her petite body to his and taking her in a passionate kiss. He'd been staring at her luscious mouth all night, watching her little pink tongue dart out to lick her lips. Instead, he bent his head to hers and gave her a chaste kiss on the cheek. He passed his nose over her hair as he drew back and inhaled deeply. She smelled of vanilla with a hint of strawberries—*fuck*, good enough to eat. He forced himself away and stepped through the door.

"Sweet dreams, Makayla." He bade her goodnight before turning and walking to his car.

Makayla shut and locked the door, then leaned against it, a surprising sadness suddenly overcoming her. Slowly, she slid to the floor. As soon as she'd mentioned her mother's problems, he'd shut down, leaving soon after. Why wouldn't he? Why would he be interested in a woman who couldn't go out, who couldn't possibly have a normal relationship? She laughed ruefully. Anyway, who said that he was even interested in a relationship? He was probably just being nice when he'd accepted her invitation to dinner. Initially, he had wanted to take her out, probably with a view toward something afterward. Then he'd asked her again and she'd had to refuse. That was it, his patience had obviously reached its peak and he was tired of her. And, no doubt, he wanted nothing to do with the problems that her mother presented. She sighed deeply. It was nice while it had lasted, she supposed. One night where she felt special—what woman wouldn't be flattered by the attention of such a man? At least, she thought, she had some fuel for her fantasies that should keep her going for a while.

She picked herself up from the floor and moved through the house, turning off lights. It didn't take her long. It was a small home—small but cozy. She yawned deeply and realized how tired she was. All the stress of the day—cooking and worrying about Donovan's visit—had finally taken its toll. She got ready for bed quickly and was asleep almost as soon as her head hit the pillow.

Chapter Six

Makayla stood frowning at the unfamiliar woman on her doorstep

The woman smiled. "Mr. King said that you would require an explanation. He obviously hasn't spoken to you about me. My name's Kathy Broadbent. These are my credentials." She handed Makayla an official-looking document. "Mr. King hired me to watch over Josephine for the evening. I'm a registered nurse. He asked that I come early so I could meet you and you could ensure that Josephine was settled before you left for the evening."

Mind reeling, Makayla mulled over the conversation with Donovan the previous evening. He had said that he would take her to dinner, and that he was accustomed to getting what he wanted—this was obviously his way of achieving that. She couldn't possibly accept. It wasn't right, and her mother would probably hate the thought of a stranger in their home. But before she could voice her opposition to the plan, her mother appeared by her side, alerted to the fact that someone was at the door.

"You must be Josephine." The woman on the doorstep smiled brightly and extended her hand. "It's lovely to meet you. I'm Kathy." At the look of confusion on her mother's face, Kathy continued, "Mr. King asked me to sit with you this evening so he can take your daughter to dinner."

Makayla jumped in. "And I was just about to tell Kathy that it isn't necessary. Her services will unfortunately not be required."

Her mother spoke up. "I agree." Then to Makayla's horror Josephine continued, "I really don't require babysitting. I *do* agree, however, that Makayla needs a night out and I know that she won't relax if I'm at home alone. So, thank you, Kathy. Won't you please come in?"

Before Makayla had a chance to protest further, Kathy had crossed the threshold, then she and Josephine were walking toward the kitchen, her mother talking about making a pot of tea.

Makayla looked at her watch—four p.m. She had three and a half hours before Donovan would be at her door. She should call him, refuse to go to dinner and rail at him for his impudence. The audacity of his actions should have angered her immensely, but she was oddly touched by his gesture. He had listened to her last night and his solution to the problem of Makayla going to dinner with him was Kathy. It was so simple for him, so easy just to hire someone. With her mother going along with the plan, Makayla could hardly refuse. Donovan had indeed secured his way. She sighed in resignation.

Crap. Another thought hit her. What the hell was she going to wear? She took off to her bedroom and for the second time in two days, she agonized in front of her wardrobe. She imagined that the restaurant

Donovan would take her to would be quite high-end and she didn't want to embarrass him. She flicked through the hangers in despair. Most of her clothes were casual at best and many had seen better days. Her gaze fell on the magenta gown hidden at the back of her wardrobe. She hadn't thought about it since the first and only time she'd worn it — at her Year Twelve Formal, five years previously. She held it against herself. It was a little large now, as she'd lost some weight, but otherwise, it could work. She had sewn it herself to her own design. Made from a fine taffeta with capped sleeves and a sweetheart neckline, the dress had a fitted bodice, the skirt falling to her ankles in a soft A-line. A satin bow in a darker shade tied around the waist. It was too long for an informal dinner and a little outdated, but a few simple alterations would change that. A frisson of excitement shot through her. She enjoyed sewing but it had been a long time since she'd sewn for the sheer pleasure and to create something just for herself.

She used their third bedroom as a sewing room. It was tiny, hardly even a room, really, but it fit her sewing table and a trunk of material, plus a small set of shelves that held her essentials. She knew what she was going to do and she set to work. She even had some of the original fabric. She never threw material away but stored it in case she needed it later.

In three hours, Makayla practically had a new dress, and she was pleased with the results. She'd decided on a vintage, 1950s style, similar to one she'd seen and admired in a magazine. She had shortened the dress to just below her knees and fashioned a petticoat from the darker satin fabric and some white tulle, ensuring that the darker edge of the petticoat showed from beneath the skirt. She'd taken it in where required and lowered the neckline. Finally, she'd made the satin belt narrower and the bow smaller. She twirled in front of the mirror and admired the way the full skirt flipped up and out. Unbelievably, she'd found a long forgotten push-up bra in her underwear drawer, so she had a nice cleavage to fill out the bodice of the dress.

Her hair had been a challenge. It was so thick and long that she generally just piled it on top of her head or wore it in a ponytail. She had decided on wearing it loose for the evening and had blow-dried it into waves that hung past her shoulders. She'd kept her makeup light—a little mascara and pink lip gloss. On her feet she wore silver, heeled sandals that she'd bought to wear with the dress five years ago. She felt feminine and pretty, and more than ready to face the night ahead.

Chapter Seven

Donovan had decided to take Makayla to Vista. It was a restaurant attached to one of his clubs with a beautiful view over the city and excellent food. They'd been greeted enthusiastically by his maître d' and shown to a private table. Donovan wanted the evening to be special and he knew that the best place he could count on for superior service was one of his own establishments.

He studied Makayla across the table as she fidgeted with her silverware. "Did I tell you how beautiful you look this evening? That dress is amazing on you. Don't shop anywhere else."

Her head shot up, a lovely rose hue staining her cheeks as she blushed. She really must learn to take a compliment. She did look stunning. The dress did remarkable things to her figure, emphasizing her pert breasts and tiny waist. She'd seemed almost doll like—too perfect to be real. And when they arrived at his restaurant, she'd drawn all eyes to her, the women staring out of envy and the men out of admiration. It gave him a curious juxtaposition of emotions—

exhilaration to have her on his arm and irritation at having her so blatantly ogled.

She smiled broadly. "Thank you. I'm glad you like it. I made it myself. Well, actually I altered it from a gown I sewed previously. This afternoon, when I realized I didn't have anything appropriate for dinner and only a few hours to do something, I improvised." She shrugged.

He shot his eyebrows up in surprise. The dress appeared to be very professionally sewn. It fit her so perfectly he should have known it was tailor-made. She really was extremely talented.

"Do you own this restaurant?" she now asked, gazing around. "The view from up here is stunning."

"Yes, I thought it appropriate to bring you here. The food is excellent and, as you noted, the view is quite spectacular."

The waiter arrived with a bottle of Bollinger champagne and oysters. He uncorked the bottle and expertly poured two glasses before retreating quietly.

"I took the liberty of ordering our first course," he murmured. "I hope you don't mind."

"Not at all. Thank you." She smiled and raised her glass. "Shall we toast?"

"To us," Donovan murmured, raising his own glass to clink with hers.

She mimicked his actions and they each took a long sip of the bubbly liquid.

Donovan busied himself preparing their oysters, squirting lemon and sprinkling pepper then adding a small spoonful of shallot vinaigrette. He passed one to Makayla. *Bon appétit,* he said.

He watched as she brought her own to her lips and tipped her head back to slide the oyster into her mouth. "Mmm, delicious," she announced then licked her lips.

Fuck, does she know how erotic that looks? He shifted uncomfortably in his seat as his growing erection pressed against the seam of his dress pants. *Christ, but this woman does things to me.* Never before had he been affected so quickly by a woman. It was unnerving to say the least.

"How many clubs do you own?" Makayla's husky voice snapped him out of his reverie.

"Five. Three in Sydney and two in Melbourne." He took a sip of champagne. "Actually, I'm heading to Spain at the end of the week. I'm thinking of opening a club in Madrid and I have some meetings set up to discuss possibilities."

She raised an eyebrow. "Why Spain?"

"My mother is Spanish. I spent a lot of time there when I was growing up. I still go there for holidays." He shrugged. "It's part of my heritage and I love Madrid."

"Do your parents live in Spain?"

"My mother comes from Mallorca, and they have a home there which they spend part of the year in. Right now, they're staying at their holiday home in Noosa. My father's retired, and they share their time between here and Spain. Neither of them likes cold weather, preferring to avoid winter if they can." He passed her another oyster. "Eat up. I love watching you swallow these."

She rewarded him with another one of her pretty blushes as she flustered with her napkin. She really acted quite delightfully when she was self-conscious, and he found he enjoyed making her feel ill at ease just to see the deep flush spread across her cheeks. He should leave her alone. His every instinct was telling him to abandon this unfamiliar courtship he was enacting and return to the easy, habitual way of doing things—no romance, just wild, raw fucking. But he couldn't do it. He had to have her. Perhaps if he scratched that itch, if he got her into bed and fucked her brains out, he could move on and forget about her—hopefully she'd be out of his system. He knew he was being an ass, but he wasn't good for her—his dark proclivities and desires were not for her world of sunshine and light. Then again, he knew that she'd make an excellent submissive. He recalled when she'd called him sir at their first meeting, and the subsequent sexual thrill that had scorched through him. He'd fantasized about tying her up and dominating her, spanking her pert little ass until it was nice and pink. Just thinking about it made his cock throb with need and he adjusted himself in his suit pants, glad of the tablecloth covering his lap. Yes, he'd love to have her submit fully to him, to have her under his complete control and domination, but he knew he wouldn't expose her to that side of his lifestyle—he couldn't. She was too innocent and he knew without a doubt that she'd never experienced anything like what he was used to doing with his partners. But there was no denying that he wanted her any way he could get her. With Makayla, that meant vanilla sex if, in fact, things progressed to that. And it was definitely what he was working toward.

He studied her across the table and wondered if he'd wooed her enough that she'd feel comfortable taking the next step.

The waiter appeared at their table. "Your chateaubriand, Mr. King." He placed a platter of delicious-looking fillet steak and sauce between them.

"Thank you. I'll serve. You can leave," Donovan informed the waiter brusquely.

"As you wish, sir." He bowed slightly before leaving them alone.

Makayla raised an eyebrow at Donovan. "You ordered our main too?"

He shrugged and smiled. "There's something intimate and sensual about sharing a meal, and besides, I know you like steak."

Warmth spread through her at his words, a ripple of desire trailing down her spine. This man was really working his way under her skin. The penetrating looks he gave her, combined with his blatant sexuality and imposing presence, both aroused her and slightly intimidated her—it was a potent combination.

She watched as he served her first then helped himself. It smelled delicious, and as she took a bite, she couldn't help the moan of pleasure that burst out of her. It tasted divine and the meat melted on her tongue. She knew she'd have no trouble finishing what was on her plate.

Donovan chuckled. "Good?"

"Absolutely," she confirmed. "I don't think I've ever sampled anything so delightful."

"I'm glad of your approval. After all, you're a fabulous cook, so your good opinion is all the more valuable."

Already she knew better than to protest his praise. She smiled weakly and looked down at her plate, still uncomfortable with his admiration. It was silly, particularly as she *knew* she was a good cook. But she found it difficult, mainly because those compliments were coming from the perfect specimen of a man opposite her—a successful, ridiculously handsome man, who could claim any woman he chose. She knew, deep down, that she felt inferior in his presence.

She quickly shook herself out of her morose thoughts, thoughts that would only serve to damage her self-confidence. Instead, she decided it was a good moment to broach the subject of the nurse that Donovan had taken upon himself to organize for her mother. She couldn't decide if she should be angry at his audacity or grateful for his thoughtfulness.

She finished her mouthful of steak, placed her knife and fork together on the plate and elected to ask him outright what his intent had been, though she suspected she already knew the answer. "Donovan, why did you organize Kathy to sit with my mother?"

He looked up at her, surprise crossing his features before he settled his expression into an implacable mask. "I wonder at you asking. You told me last night that Josephine is unwell, that you dislike leaving her alone for any extended period. And I told you that I always find a way to get what I want. I wanted you, alone and having dinner with me. Organizing a nurse to sit with your mother seemed like an obvious solution."

"You didn't think to ask first?"

He frowned. "No, because I know that you would have refused and that would have made me mad. I was also sure that once Josephine understood my intentions, she would agree readily enough. I didn't see a problem and I wanted you relaxed and free from distraction. Do you agree that you haven't worried about your mother while we've been sharing this meal?"

"Yes," she conceded guiltily. It was the fact that Kathy was a professional, and her mother had been having some good days of late that had eased

Makayla's mind. Also, her mum had seemed genuinely pleased to have some company, a woman other than Makayla and Mrs. Young to talk to.

"Thank you. It was a generous gesture and very thoughtful of you."

He gave her a devilish grin. "I believe that I had quite a self-serving motive, but I appreciate your gratitude." He looked at her plate with satisfaction. "You've eaten everything. I'm glad. You're too slender. That's another plus to my plan—it gave you an appetite."

She smiled. "Well, it was simply too delicious to pass up. Even I'm surprised at my appetite, Mr. King."

He cleared his throat. "Are you ready to leave? I thought we'd have dessert at my place."

Chapter Eight

Makayla was unsurprised that Donovan owned a penthouse overlooking Sydney Harbor. Its main theme was black, gray and white neutrals—sophisticated but too austere for Makayla's tastes. She loved color and attitude. Donovan's home had clearly been designed for the bachelor that he was—masculine and straightforward.

He'd organized more champagne and had a bowl of strawberries and chocolate truffles ready and waiting. Numerous candles illuminated the lounge, giving the area a soft, sensual feel. Everything about the evening, Makayla realized, was about seduction—the oysters, the shared chateaubriand, and now the fruit and champagne.

Makayla took in the room and the romantic gestures. She hoped that it meant that Donovan had the same thing on his mind as she had on hers. She wanted him desperately. She'd never felt so sexually aroused by a man, so wantonly desirous. If she had to choose a man to take away her V card, Donovan would be *the* one. Surely, he wouldn't have gone to the trouble that he had if he didn't want to sleep with her? No, she was sure that tonight was the night she would finally learn what all the fuss was about. She'd wanted to experience sex for a long time, but circumstances hadn't allowed it. Tonight was different. She knew her mother was in capable hands. Makayla wasn't concerned or distracted. The nurse, Kathy, had her number as well as Donovan's.

Makayla wanted to feel the physical comfort of someone else and to experience the acts that she'd read about. She wanted to feel Donovan's cock inside her as he thrust hard and fast—she wanted *him*.

Donovan pointed to the lounge. "Sit."

She sat where he asked and couldn't help but fidget. She realized that she didn't know how to do sexy or sensual. She felt awkward and a little out of her element.

He sat by her and handed her a glass of champagne. She took the offering, grateful to have something to keep her busy, and reached for a strawberry. The sweet, luscious fruit burst on her tongue, flooding her mouth with its delicate flavor.

She tried to relax into the seat and took another sip of champagne, the alcohol helping to ease her nerves. She watched Donovan over the rim of her glass as he helped himself to a strawberry. He looked utterly cool and relaxed, the epitome of controlled dignity, while she felt like a bundle of nerves. Her tummy was doing that erratic trembling again and she took another sip of her drink to try to quell the sensation. Her palms felt clammy and a slight tremor had taken hold of her limbs. She placed her glass on the coffee table and clasped her hands together in her lap. What was wrong with her? She was acting like a scared little rabbit. She cast a surreptitious look at Donovan under lowered lashes to see that he was studying her intently.

He took her hands in his much larger ones and squeezed gently. "Why are you nervous?"

"I'm not, really," she lied. "I think it's the champagne making me jittery."

He narrowed his eyes at her. "Can I ask how many men you've been with?"

Her face heated. She was embarrassed that he'd asked such a question, but more mortified by the answer. She could lie to him but the truth would present itself. He'd find out soon enough. She just hoped that her response wouldn't send him packing. He would be used to sophisticated, experienced women, women who understood their bodies and knew how to use them. That was the principal reason for her nerves — she was afraid that he'd find her lack of experience inconvenient and more trouble than was worth his time.

"Answer me," he demanded softly.

She couldn't look at him and instead stared into her lap. "None," she whispered. "I'm a virgin."

He inhaled sharply and she glanced up at him to find his expression incredulous.

"I don't fucking believe it," he said, shoving a hand through his hair. "No one at all?"

She shook her head. "Believe me, I'm keen to rid myself of my V card. It's not because I'm frigid," she hurried to assure him. "It's just that with my life the way it is..." She waved a hand in the air. "I haven't had the opportunity."

He leaned back in his chair and studied her thoughtfully, one arm draped casually across the back of the seat.

She squirmed under his intense gaze. *What is he thinking?*

Suddenly, he closed the distance between them, his powerful thigh flush against her own, his skin warm through the fabric of his pants.

He cupped her chin and turned her head to face him. She had to look up to see into his eyes, eyes swimming with lust. She held her breath as he bent his head to hers and took her lips in a passionate kiss. She melted under him, her pulse thrumming in her ears as he slipped his tongue into her mouth to tangle lazily with hers. She moaned and pressed against his hard chest, her nipples puckering in response. He trailed a hand down her side then cupped her ass to anchor her more closely to his body, deepening the kiss. She gave herself over to him totally, allowing him to manipulate her to his will, leaving her feeling giddy and lightheaded. Moisture pooled between her thighs as desire ignited within her. She felt like she was swimming in a lust-induced haze. Nothing else mattered, just the feel of his firm lips on hers, his tongue sweeping through her mouth and his muscular body, hard and unyielding, against her softer, smaller one.

She whimpered when he pulled away and swept a trail of kisses from her jaw to her ear then dropped his lips lower to suckle the tender flesh of her neck. Goosebumps flared across her skin and her nipples rose into stiff points that she was sure he'd feel through his shirt. As if in answer to her wayward thoughts, he drew a hand up her side until he found a nipple and massaged it with his thumb, his movements mimicking those of his mouth as he sucked on her throat.

She arched her head back to give him better access and pushed her breast harder into his hand, lifting hers to the nape of his neck and pulling him against her. Her breath was coming in quick bursts, her mind swamped with arousal. Oh God, if he could do this to her with just a kiss, what else could he do?

Slowly he drew away and gazed at her from under hooded lids, still using his thumb to massage little circles around her taut nipple.

"Well, I think we can safely say that you most definitely are not frigid, Miss Carrington." He chuckled. "Are you still with me?"

Makayla tried to regain her composure. She lay sprawled on the seat next to Donovan in a panting, unladylike heap. She sat up straight and fixed her dress from where it had ridden up her thighs. She didn't miss Donovan's heated gaze as he followed her movements, so she found herself drawing the act out, taking longer than necessary to smooth her dress down. The desire in his eyes gave her a powerful feeling, knowing that she had put that look there. She dropped her gaze to his lap and stared, mesmerized, at the significant bulge there—she wanted to feel it. She reached a tentative hand toward him, but he took it in his, halting her movement.

"Not so fast, my sweet," he murmured, then kissed the palm of her hand. "That's enough for tonight."

"W-what?" Flabbergasted, Makayla wondered why he wouldn't want to take things further. Was it something she'd done?

"Don't pout," he ordered. "I'm flattered that you want me as much as I want you, but you've had too much champagne. Plus, there's a certain thrill to denying ourselves. Delayed gratification does wonders to sexual intensity. I'll take you, of that you can be sure, and I'll enjoying doing it—immensely. Just not tonight."

"Oh," was all she could manage to say. She wasn't sure about delayed gratification, but she'd trust that Donovan knew what he wanted.

He stood swiftly and held a hand out toward her. "Come, I'll take you home."

Chapter Nine

Donovan could tell that Makayla had been both surprised and disappointed by his actions. In truth, he'd surprised himself. He'd wanted nothing more than to sink balls deep into that sweet, compliant body. But discovering that she was a virgin had stopped him dead. Fuck, nothing much surprised him anymore, but that revelation certainly had. He'd suspected that she wasn't very experienced, but he could have been knocked over by a feather when he found out just *how* inexperienced she was. Oddly, it had pleased him. It appealed to his possessive nature to know that no other man had had her before him, that he would be the first. He'd make damn sure of that too. He'd had to adjust his plans a little but the thought of waiting for her was as appealing as it was frustrating. Plus, she'd been a little tipsy from the champagne and he wasn't a complete bastard—there was no way he wanted her first time to consist of blurred memories. He wanted her to remember everything. She'd responded to him so perfectly. She'd turned into putty in his arms, letting him take control of their kiss and practically swooning beneath him. Yes, she would be perfect for him, and waiting to fuck her would be sweet torture. He'd left her on her doorstep with strict instructions not to touch herself. She'd rewarded him with a fierce blush then a look of pure confusion. He hadn't elaborated as to why he didn't want her to masturbate. He knew instinctively that she'd do as he requested.

Now he was making plans to take her to Madrid with him. It was crazy. Hell, they'd only just met, but he was going to be tied up in meetings all week and he'd have no time to see Makayla before he left. He knew it was irrational, but he had the fear that if he went to Madrid without her, she'd find someone in his absence. She now seemed to be intent on losing her V card, as she'd so eloquently put it, and there was no way he would allow anyone else to have that honor. No, he'd make the arrangements and do everything in his power to convince her to accompany him.

* * * *

Makayla sat staring at the package that had arrived while she was out shopping. It had been two days since she'd seen Donovan. He'd dropped her at home after they'd had dinner and that was the last she'd heard from him. She'd been afraid that she *had* scared him off. It was hardly surprising, he had a raw and virile sexuality that would have women jumping into bed with him, so what on earth would he do with a silly little virgin? Thankfully, it looked like she'd been mistaken, because she knew this package was from him, and unless it was a 'thanks, but no thanks,' it could only mean that Donovan was still interested in her.

She tore into the package and fished out an envelope. Inside lay a doctor's certificate, stating that Donovan was of perfect health and free from STDs. She read the document in confusion. Why would Donovan send her his medical status? Then it hit her—he wanted to assure her that he was safe to be with. It was considerate of him, but he hadn't asked her about her medical status. What if she'd had a blood transfusion or she was an intravenous drug user? There was nothing for him to worry about, but she'd assure him at any rate. Now, she was positive. She had confirmation—Donovan did want to take things further.

Just as she was contemplating Donovan's intentions, a knock sounded at the door. She opened it to find a deliveryman surrounded by packages.

"Miss Makayla Carrington?"

"Yes."

"Delivery for you. Sign here, please."

The man carried everything into the hallway and handed her an envelope. "Have a nice day," he told her as he stepped over the threshold and walked swiftly to his van.

Makayla surveyed the numerous boxes and bags in dismay. She opened one package and looked inside to find a strappy sundress. Others held camisoles and tops, shorts and more dresses. Another possessed lingerie, yet another contained swimsuits. In the boxes, nestled in tissue paper, she discovered a dozen pairs of shoes. Everything was in her size. How had he achieved this?

She couldn't believe it. Why would Donovan purchase all of these clothes for her? She couldn't accept them, of course. It was inappropriate and far too expensive. She'd forgotten all about the letter she'd discarded on the hall table. Now she ripped into the new missive to see what Donovan had to say for himself.

Dearest Makayla,

It would make me very happy for you to accept the clothes, and it will give me great pleasure to see you in something that I bought for you. Think of it as a selfish gift to myself.

You need to pack and be ready to fly out of Sydney on Friday evening. Our plane leaves at ten p.m. I'm still unsure as to the duration of our stay, so you need to be flexible.

I'll be in touch with further details.

Yours,

Donovan

"Is he crazy?" She had to speak to him before he took this madness any further, and he hadn't even asked her the most basic of things, like did she have a passport? She did, but she'd never used it. She'd obtained it for a trip with her grandparents, then her mother had grown too unwell to be left alone. She grabbed Donovan's card from her purse and dialed his mobile number, not caring if she was interrupting his workday.

He answered on the fourth ring. "King."

"Donovan, it's Makayla."

"Ah, you've received the gifts and my letter, then?"

"Yes," she said with exasperation. "But you know I can't go traipsing off to Madrid with you. I can't leave my mother alone for any length of time. And the clothes and shoes are far too much, Donovan. Also, how do you even know I have a passport, and how could you book me a ticket without it? I can't go with you." She was panting heavily into the phone, breathless from her outburst.

"Are you finished?"

His cold, disembodied voice reached down the line and sent shivers rippling through her.

"Yes," she whispered, suddenly a little contrite.

"Of course I wouldn't expect you to go away and leave your mother. I spoke to Josephine's doctor about the best treatment facility for her and I've booked her into it. They're expecting her on Friday morning."

"What?" Makayla screeched into the phone. How on earth could he have spoken to her mother's doctor?

"I talked to Josephine and she gave her doctor permission to speak to me," he explained smoothly. "She also told me your dress and shoe size and your passport details. Don't make this more difficult than it is. I wanted to buy you things, as I said in my note — it will give *me* pleasure to see you wearing them. Unfortunately, they're not nearly as beautiful as what you could make, but time is limited and I don't want you slaving over a sewing machine. You need these things for the plans I have in Madrid."

Makayla was reeling. Was there no end to what Donovan would do to get what he wanted? And what did her mother think about all this? She definitely hadn't mentioned anything to Makayla. Booking into a treatment facility was a big deal. What if her mum didn't like it there?

"I'm not sure," she finally murmured. "This is all happening so quickly. I need to think about it."

He sighed down the phone. "There's nothing to think about, Makayla. Everything's been settled. Talk to your mother. She'll tell you that she's happy with the arrangements." He paused. "Did you get my other letter?"

"Your doctor's certificate? Yes, I did."

"Good. Are you on birth control? If not, I want you to start straight away."

She couldn't believe they were having this conversation. Then again, it was probably easier for her to discuss these things when she couldn't see him. "As it happens," she muttered, "and it's really none of your business, but I am on birth control to regulate my periods."

"Excellent and you're wrong—it's very much my business. Look, I have to go into a meeting. Start packing and remember it's summer in Madrid. I'll talk to you later."

Makayla stared at the phone after Donovan had hung up. She felt like she was in an alternate universe and she'd just been run over with a bulldozer named Donovan King. She needed to speak to her mother. It appeared that she knew a hell of a lot more about what was going on than Makayla did.

Chapter Ten

The rest of the week flew by and Friday came upon Makayla quickly. She could hardly believe that she was actually going away to Madrid, and with Donovan King, no less.

She had taken her mother to the treatment facility, and had been immensely relieved when they'd arrived to find a lovely hospital with beautiful grounds. Her mother had a private room and all the staff seemed professional and very friendly. Also, the facility was highly recommended by her mum's doctor and had an excellent success rate. It seemed that Donovan's parents contributed a sizeable donation each year that assisted low-income patients, and one call to the board of directors had got her mum an immediate placement. Makayla should have felt guilty for bumping someone off the list, but her mother was ill and in desperate need of professional attention, so she consoled herself rather easily.

Now they were comfortably ensconced in their first-class seats, sipping champagne. Makayla felt overwhelmed by all the events of the week. Her stomach was tied in knots and she couldn't quite believe that she was going away with a man she had only just met.

Their seats were located a little farther apart than she'd expected, but such was the layout of first class and their private cubicles. She was happy for the time alone to think, and soon enough, they'd be spending a lot of time together. Donovan, in a seat a little ahead of hers, lounged comfortably while reading through a document.

Makayla hadn't missed the flight attendant's interest in him. She'd been extremely professional, of course, but her furtive glances and wide smile hadn't gone unnoticed — at least not by Makayla. And it didn't help that the flight attendant was tall and beautiful and obviously worldly — totally Donovan's type.

She sipped more champagne and nibbled on hors d'oeuvres that the flight attendants had served.

What she was doing was quite reckless. What did she really know about this man? Surprisingly, her mother had thought the exact opposite of him. *She* had been excited that Makayla had the opportunity to go away with a man as handsome and successful as Donovan. He'd managed to charm Josephine so much that she could see no wrong in him.

Makayla *did* have a security fallback. She had a small amount of money that she'd saved over the years, and it would be enough to get her back to Australia should the need arise. It gave her a feeling of assurance to know that she wasn't totally at the mercy of Donovan's desires, and if things between them didn't work out, she had an escape option. She hoped with everything in her being that she wouldn't have to use it. She had no idea where Donovan wanted their relationship to go, if in fact that was what it was, but she'd take things day by day and enjoy the moment. She'd live carefree for a time and enjoy doing it. He was no doubt classing their trip together as a fling. Perhaps he had an itch to scratch. Was it the challenge to get a virgin in the sack? Although, if that's all it was to him, he was definitely pulling out all the stops. If she were honest, she hoped that he wanted more than just a fling, because *she* definitely wanted more. She yawned, overcome with weariness, the hectic week having finally caught up with her. Perhaps she could close her eyes for a little while. After all, they had fourteen hours before they touched down in Dubai. She had plenty of time to catch up on some sleep.

Donovan hadn't spoken to Makayla since they'd boarded the plane, and he wanted to assure himself that she was all right. She'd been quiet leading up to the flight and he hadn't had much time to spend with her beforehand. He knew his actions to get her where he wanted her would seem manipulative and high-handed to the most easygoing of people. But that's how he was used to doing things. He liked control, he liked getting what he wanted and he did everything in his power to make it happen. He just hoped that he hadn't overwhelmed her with his officiousness.

He packed away the documents he'd been reading and unlatched his seatbelt. They'd reached cruising altitude a while ago and the seatbelt sign had been switched off. He made his way to Makayla's seat and stood over her sleeping form. She lay curled up in the large airline seat like a kitten, her thick eyelashes fanning against her pale cheekbones. She was so lovely, even more so because she didn't realize it and didn't play on her beauty. She was guileless and perfectly sweet with it. When he'd picked her up to take her to the airport, he'd been gratified to see her wearing the clothes that he'd purchased for her. Black leggings, boots and an oversized, deep amethyst silk blouse. He'd instructed the personal shopper to include shades of blue and purple in her selections, as Donovan loved the way the colors brought out the amazing violet of Makayla's eyes.

There had been a moment when he'd thought that all his planning would be for nought and that Makayla would refuse to accompany him. Josephine had called him and said that Makayla was being particularly stubborn. In the end, they'd succeeded in talking her round. He knew in part that it was because Josephine had been having a good week. If she'd had one of her downturns, Donovan wasn't sure that he would have convinced Makayla to leave her mother, even if it was at one of the best treatment facilities in the country. At any rate, he'd breathed a deep sigh of relief when he finally had Makayla packed up and in the car.

He dropped a hand to her head to brush the wayward tendrils from her brow. Fuck, he was having a hard time not touching her. Never had he wanted anything more than to be in her sweet little panties. The waiting was torturing him, but he'd decided that he wanted everything to be perfect. He needed her to be comfortable with him and to enjoy the experience. He'd always prided himself on his self-control. It was what made him who he was, after all, but he had to admit that it was taking every ounce of willpower not to dive on her. It had helped that he'd been busy all week.

The flight attendant appeared at his side. "We'll be serving a late dinner soon, sir," she informed him, smiling widely.

"Nothing for the moment, thank you. We'll have something later."

Her smile faltered as she looked from him to Makayla. Donovan was aware that she'd been flirting with him, even though she'd hidden it under a professional veneer. He wasn't arrogant. He was just used to the way women reacted to him.

"Of course, sir." She gave him a brittle smile. "Can I get you anything now?"

"Just a blanket, thank you."

He leaned down and unclipped Makayla's belt then gently lifted her so he could slide into her place. He settled her on his lap. She really was too slight and he hoped that some Spanish food and a holiday would be good for her appetite. She hardly stirred at the intrusion, just nuzzled against his chest and mumbled something in her sleep. He reclined the seat until they were lying flat and tucked her tighter against his chest. It wasn't like him to want to sleep with a woman cuddled in his arms. In fact, he couldn't remember ever doing it before. Usually, he preferred his own space and always slept alone, but he was enjoying having her close to him, and he relished the fact that he'd have her to himself for the foreseeable future.

Chapter Eleven

Makayla plastered her face against the window of the limousine. There was so much to see that she was afraid she'd miss something.

Donovan chuckled. "You know, angel, the city will be here tomorrow."

"I'm so excited," she enthused, jumping a little in her seat. "I can't wait to start exploring."

She was glad to have arrived finally. The flight had been long and had included a three-hour stopover in Dubai, where they'd had a shower in the lounge facilities, and she'd changed into a sundress. She'd also washed and dried her hair and shaved everywhere. She didn't know what Donovan had planned, but she didn't want to be caught unawares and in need of some personal grooming—that would be mortifying.

She'd flown before on a few occasions—however, only within Australia, and definitely never the distance they'd just traveled. She was a little tired, but the excitement of her new surroundings outweighed any residual weariness. Besides, it was early in Madrid, approaching midday, and she'd slept well on the plane. She'd been surprised and delighted to wake up in Donovan's arms. It had seemed a little out of character for him, he didn't seem like the type of guy who liked to snuggle, particularly in public, but she wouldn't complain, she had felt comfortable and safe with him. She'd also liked the fact that the flirty flight attendant seemed to have her nose firmly out of joint when Donovan paid no attention to her and made it quite clear to her that Makayla was the object of his affections.

Donovan took her hand in his. "We're staying at the Totally Five Star Madrid. You'll love it. It's opposite *Parque del Buen Retiro,* or simply *El Retiro* to the locals, and it's part of the best hotel chain that Madrid — or anywhere else in the world — has to offer."

"Will we be staying in the same room?" she asked innocently.

He narrowed his eyes at her. "I've only booked the one room. Does that bother you?"

"Not at all. I'd started to think that something was wrong with me," she confessed.

He lifted her hand to his lips and kissed her palm. "I told you, angel. It's all about delayed gratification."

She eyed him curiously. "How's that working for you?"

He shifted in his seat then leaned down to speak in her ear. "It's torture. I can't wait to get into your panties."

She giggled. Something about their new environment was making her unusually flirtatious. "You mean these panties?" she asked coyly as she lifted her dress to show the champagne-colored silk she was wearing.

"Fuck, baby," he groaned. "You can't do that to me."

He grasped her dress and pulled it back down over her thighs. "Trust me," he said softly, stroking her knee with his index finger. "Let me do things my way."

She sighed. "I suppose I've waited this long—a little longer is hardly going to worry me."

"We're here," Donovan announced.

The limousine pulled to a stop in front of a very impressive-looking building.

"It looks like a palace," Makayla breathed in awe. "It's beautiful."

Donovan smiled. "It did use to be a palace. You will see lots of noble features reminiscent of its royal heritage."

She stepped from the car and gazed around. Large, ornate pillars and two marble lions framed the grand double entrance doors inlaid with beveled glass. Petunias flowed in colorful abundance from the numerous window boxes, their unusual scent making Makayla instantly reminisce about summers past. Even the fierce little gargoyles perched in varying degrees across the edifice provided a charming addition. A doorman, in full livery, guarded the entry, opening doors and hailing taxis. A pristine red carpet covered the steps, lending a celebrity-like status to guests and leading them into the opulent lobby.

"Come." Donovan took her arm and led her into the hotel. Instead of a front check-in desk, he guided her to a lounge suite upholstered in a rich floral satin.

"Mr. King, welcome back," a tall, attractive gentleman in a crisp suit greeted Donovan enthusiastically. "Please, help yourself to some refreshments." He motioned to a tray with tea, juice and pastries on the table in front of them.

"Thank you, Fernando. I'm happy to be back." Donovan turned to Makayla. "May I introduce Miss Makayla Carrington? She'll be staying with me. Makayla, this is *Señor* Fernando Martínez, the manager here."

Fernando bowed slightly and took her hand. "*Encantado, señorita*. Welcome to the Totally Five Star. I'm the manager here, so please let me know if anything is not to your liking."

"Thank you. But I'm sure everything will be perfect."

Fernando turned to Donovan. "Your usual suite is ready, Mr. King. I just need to finalize some details with you."

While Donovan spoke with the manager, Makayla surveyed the glorious refreshments laid out for them. Cut crystal carafes held water and juice, beside them matching tumblers. A three-tiered ceramic cake stand displayed lovely bite-sized morsels of pastries and little finger sandwiches. Dainty matching plates with heavy damask napkins were laid out neatly next to it. The care and attention to detail was extraordinary, and Makayla had never seen anything like it before. It made her feel special and important. She poured herself a glass of juice and took a sip. It was freshly squeezed orange juice and the flavor was fruity and intense. She'd read that Valencia oranges were the best in the world and she was willing to bet that it was from those oranges she was now partaking. She selected a pastry and a finger sandwich and nibbled on each. The sandwich was prawn salad with watercress and tasted divine. She thought that the pastry was what they called churros, but had been made finger-sized to assist with dainty eating and tasted a little like an upmarket donut.

As she ate and sipped her juice, she studied their surroundings. Everything was so grand as to be a little intimidating. Large white and black marble tiles covered the entirety of the lobby floor and a grand piano sat in a corner, polished so highly that she was sure she would see her reflection in the wood. All the fittings were brass, also buffed to a high shine, and antique tables held beautiful, ornate vases that sprouted an exotic array of perfumed orchids. Comfortable, overstuffed armchairs upholstered in rich fabrics sat grouped around the lobby, offering guests private areas to chat and read, and large tapestries depicting different stages in royal history and hunting scenes adorned the walls.

A marble fountain constructed of frolicking sea nymphs, surrounded by a circle of lions, took center stage. The tinkling water providing a whimsical backdrop to the light classical music transmitted throughout the lobby via seemingly invisible speakers.

Above them hung the most magnificent chandelier that she'd ever seen. Composed of thousands of crystal teardrops, the fixture sent fractured light bouncing off the walls around them and sparkling in the fountain's surface.

She glanced over to where Donovan and Fernando were deep in muted conversation. She couldn't understand a thing as they were speaking Spanish. She should have guessed that Donovan would be proficient in the language.

Donovan switched to English and stood to shake the other man's hand. "Thank you, Fernando."

"My pleasure, Mr. King. Your luggage has been delivered to your suite. Miss Carrington" — he took Makayla's hand in his own and raised it to his lips — "it was a pleasure to meet you."

She smiled her thanks, then Donovan quickly reclaimed her, wrapping an arm around her waist and tugging her to his side. Makayla was a little taken aback by Donovan's seemingly domineering gesture, but Fernando just smiled benignly.

"We offer many things to amuse, entertain and relax, Miss Carrington. At six-thirty each evening, there is live piano music here in the lobby where you can also take *tapas* and *cava*. You will find the Rococo Bar here on the ground floor along with an Asian fusion restaurant. On the top floor, you will find the Five Star Terrace Bar and our three-star Michelin restaurant, which offers a spectacular view of Madrid, and where you can sample specialty Spanish cuisine. There are two outdoor pools and an indoor pool attached to our spa and health facility. We have numerous gyms offering the use of equipment and personal trainers and we provide daily yoga classes. You must browse our boutique located at the far end of the lobby. And if you are interested in doing any traveling or perhaps a tour of our lovely city, just ask your personal butler and he shall organize anything you desire."

"Thank you, Fernando. Miss Carrington will have ample time to sample the delights that the hotel has to offer," Donovan responded. "If you'll excuse us, please. It's been a long flight and we'd like to freshen up."

The manager smiled and gestured toward the lifts. "Of course. I hope you enjoy your stay with us."

Donovan swept a hand from her waist down to her ass and cupped her butt cheek as he urged her toward the elevator bank. She gave him a side look. Donovan *definitely* wasn't the type of guy to go for PDA, so why the whole possessive attitude?

They stopped at the elevators where Donovan punched in a sequence of numbers. "We're staying in one of the penthouse suites," he said in explanation to her questioning look.

The lift arrived and they stepped inside, the doors gliding silently closed behind them. Donavan stepped closer to her and urged her against the wall of the car, his hands coming up to rest on either side of her head, caging her in as he dipped his head toward hers.

"Are you tired?" he asked, his voice husky and low.

Crazy butterflies sprang to life deep in Makayla's belly and a shiver rippled down her spine. "No," she breathed.

He smirked and dropped his lips to her ear. "Good, because I have a surprise for you when we get to our suite. It's time. I can't fucking wait any longer."

Chapter Twelve

When Donovan opened the door to their suite, the most pungent floral scent hit Makayla. As she stepped over the threshold, the first thing she saw were flowers—bunches of them scattered throughout the rooms in crystal vases and ceramic urns, their summer aroma providing a lovely romantic mood. Filmy gauze curtains fluttered in the warm breeze flowing through the open balcony doors. The decorating theme appeared to be an eclectic mix of old and new, which the decorator had managed with finesse. The whole ambience of the suite appealed to Makayla's creative designer side, and she guessed that the interior decorator was extremely accomplished to be able to pull off such a combination. The plush carpet boasted a big floral motif that worked well in the large rooms. Crystal ornaments were scattered about on sideboards. Antique trunks and suitcases were stacked on top of each other and used as tables with contemporary original artwork hanging above. A large beveled mirror hung above the mantelpiece, reflecting the room and adding an opulent quality.

The whole décor screamed understated sophistication, and she knew instinctively that every item within had been handpicked for a specific purpose and was probably worth more than she'd make in a lifetime.

On a teak table in the middle of the sitting room sat a platter of fresh fruit and cheese. Next to it, in a silver bucket, a bottle of wine chilled. One of her favorite Nina Simone albums was playing softly in the background — how did he know she loved that artist?

Makayla gasped in delight. Everything was so enchanting and so romantic. She was speechless. She spun around, arms out in elation and excitement.

She looked at Donovan, who leaned against the doorway, watching her in amusement.

"Donovan, this is so wonderful," she cried breathlessly.

He moved quickly, suddenly by her side, grasping her around the waist and pulling her body tight into his. "Do you like it, baby?" he breathed against her ear.

"I love it." She threw her arms about his shoulders. "And you said that you're not romantic," she admonished. "This is seriously romantic, Mr. King."

He dropped his head to her neck and inhaled deeply. "I did say that, sweet girl." He muttered against her throat. "But that was until I met you." He lifted his head so he was looking into her eyes. "You've done strange things to me, Miss Carrington. And now I want to do strange things to *you*."

He took her hand and led her to the bathroom. She gaped yet again in surprise. The enormous bathtub was filled with water and rose petals floated on the surface. The windows and shades were open, allowing the summer breeze to waft in, giving an open-air quality to the room. The view of *El Retiro* spread like a miniature garden below.

She met Donovan's heated gaze and immediately her nipples puckered in response and her belly fluttered wildly.

"Take off your clothes, Makayla," he demanded in a soft voice. "I've waited too fucking long to see that perfect body."

She hesitated, the quivering in her belly turning into churning turmoil.

"I don't want to ask twice, baby," he said, a roguish smile curving his lips.

She kicked off her sandals and slowly drew the sundress up and over her head. She tossed it aside and stood before him in champagne-colored silk and lace lingerie. She lifted her gaze to his, immediately reassured by the raw lust shining from his eyes. He wanted her—badly—and the realization made her feel sexy and confident.

Slowly he moved toward her, reached up and drew his thumb over her puckered nipple. "So beautiful," he muttered hoarsely. "So fucking perfect."

He cupped her breast over the silk, and massaged the tight nub with his thumb. She closed her eyes and moaned, arching into him and pressing herself against his hand. Liquid heat pooled between her thighs and weightlessness suffused her limbs as she succumbed to his touch.

Then suddenly his touch was gone and she was bereft. "Take it off," he ordered, indicating her bra.

She quickly unclasped it and shrugged the lace down her shoulders and off her arms. She tossed it to join her dress on the floor, the movement making her breasts bounce.

"Fuck," he snarled, reclaiming her breast and pinching the nipple roughly.

"Ahh," she moaned. A pleasurable pain shot through her straight to her clit, and she bowed toward him.

He dropped his left hand to her lower back, and she arched further, savoring the rhythmic massaging of her breast and nipple.

"Open your eyes, angel. I want to see their beautiful violet."

Languidly, she fluttered her eyelids open and gazed up at him. He was studying her intently, gauging her reaction to his touch. He released her breast and slid his hand slowly down her torso, the sensation sending shivers rippling through her. When he reached her panties, she groaned, her legs opening automatically to allow him access, her eyelids fluttering closed of their own accord.

"Keep your eyes open," he grated between clenched teeth.

She opened her eyes wide and met his heated stare.

"That's it," he coaxed. "I need to *see* your response to me."

When he reached inside her panties, she held her breath. He found her folds and slipped his finger inside, lightly massaging her passage. She groaned and thrust her hips up against his hand.

"So fucking wet," he grunted. "A wet, aroused virgin, and so fucking tight." His pupils dilated and he licked his lips. "You're going to be the death of me."

He slid his finger out and ran her moisture over the lips of her pussy, finding her clit and pressing down.

She cried out and jerked against him. He tightened his arm at her back and pulled her body tighter to his as he slid his finger back inside and pushed it deeper.

"Oh God," she cried. Tremors wracked her and she breathed deeply, working through the pleasure-pain that Donovan was wreaking on her body.

"I want you to come like this, Makayla, and I want to see it in your beautiful eyes."

She focused her blurry vision on him and opened her legs wider as he cupped her sex. The heel of his palm provided friction to her clit as he pushed another finger inside her and pumped them in and out slowly. It wasn't deep and the small pain was bearable.

The squelching sounds of her own arousal filled the room and she tried to close her legs, suddenly mortified.

"Don't," he demanded.

His knowing smirk told her he understood exactly what she was thinking.

"Hear how wet you are! Can you smell your arousal? It's. So. Fucking. Hot."

He thrust higher and deeper. She felt a twinge of pain but the pleasure that was pulsing through her body overpowered everything else. She moaned and propelled her hips in time with his pumping fingers.

"That's it, angel. Keep looking at me."

He circled her clit with his thumb and pressed down.

Her vision hazed, she stiffened in his arms and cried out. Suddenly the pulsing pleasure coalesced into a wave of sensation, centering on her core then undulating outward in a slow, throbbing swell.

Donovan slowed the thrust of his fingers, gentling the pressure and working her slowly through her climax.

She trembled as her orgasm receded, leaving her weak and lightheaded. Never had she been able to achieve such a powerful release by her own hand. *Jesus, the man is obviously a sexual king — king by name, king by nature.*

"You are too much, Makayla," he breathed. "Watching you come in my arms was the most erotic thing I've ever seen. A quaking, wet, climaxing virgin. I almost came just watching you."

She gazed up into his lust-filled eyes and blushed in dismay as he lifted his fingers to his lips and sucked them into his mouth. "And you taste so fucking good."

She realized that she was still supported by his arm and she struggled to right herself, worried that she was causing him pain.

"What are you doing?" he demanded. "Stop wriggling." He swept her up, cradling her in his arms, and deposited her in the tub.

"Remove your panties and lie back and relax," he ordered.

Makayla shimmied quickly out of her underwear and lowered herself into the warm, fragrant water. She smirked at him. "Are you always this bossy and controlling?"

He grinned. "Always. Get used to it."

She gave him a pointed look. "You're still fully clothed and I'm naked and the only one in the bath."

"I know. I'm afraid that if I get in there with you, I won't be able to stop myself from taking you hard and fast."

"And what's wrong with that?"

"That's not how I want to do things. I'm so hard right now that I think I could cut glass with my cock, and you need to relax. I want you soft and pliable before I fuck you."

She gasped at his crassness and he chuckled.

"Lie back, I want to bathe you."

She did as he asked and rested her head on the back of the tub, closing her eyes. He squeezed water over her breasts. He inhaled sharply, then his mouth was at her ear. "I have the best view at the moment. I'm looking at two of the most perfect breasts I've ever seen and thinking that I can't wait to take those rosy-pink nipples into my mouth and suck them — hard."

"Hmm, I can't wait for you to do that," she murmured, thrusting her breasts up and out of the water, hoping to coax him into action sooner rather than later.

She peeked up at him but he was ignoring her blatant tease and rubbing soap to a lather between his hands. Then he grasped her shoulders and started to massage.

"You need to be relaxed to minimize the pain when I take you." He dipped his head and nibbled on the flesh beneath her ear, sending sharp tingles straight to her aching nipples.

"Then again," he mused, still nuzzling her throat, "I do like the fact that you're a virgin. Perhaps I'll keep you like that. There's something so fucking erotic about making you wet and watching you climax but knowing your hymen's still intact — that you're still pure."

She pulled away and turned her head to glare at him. "I'm not keeping my V card so you can appease some weird, kinky virgin fetish you have." She narrowed her eyes at him. "That's not why you asked me to come here with you, is it? Because you have an obsession with my virginity?"

He threw his head back and laughed. "No, I haven't given it much thought. It's only now, when I have a wet, soapy, delicious specimen in front of me, that it appeals. And to be honest, I like the fact that when I take you, I'll have a part of you, a part that no one else can have again. Once it's gone—it's gone." He shrugged. "I've been drawing out the anticipation of finally taking you, as well as delaying my satisfaction."

"And mine," she grumbled.

He ignored her. "Of course, there's also a twisted delight in knowing that no other man has been there before me."

"I'm not a planet," she said petulantly.

He grinned. "No, more like a star, a star that I'll enjoy conquering immensely."

She shook her head in exasperation. "You are one kinky so-and-so."

"More than you know," he said under his breath.

But she caught the words anyway.

He swept his hands over her breasts, down her sides and parted her legs, holding them firmly against the sides of the tub. "Wash that sweet little pussy for me," he whispered in her ear. Her breath hitched and she grasped the bar of soap, lathering the washcloth then sweeping it through her folds while Donovan continued holding her thighs firmly open. It was sensual and erotic, washing so intimately while he watched. His breathing grew heavy and hot in her ear as she tended to her herself.

"That's enough," he said hoarsely. "My self control is deserting me." He dunked a washcloth in the tub and swept it over her shoulders and clavicle, ridding her of any residual soap. "Now, out of the tub."

He grasped her around the waist, hauled her up then lowered her to the bath mat. He grabbed a fluffy white towel and started rubbing her down. Funny, but she'd lost any residual shyness and stood complacently, allowing him to towel her dry. She could have dried herself, of course, but she let Donovan do whatever made him happy. She glanced down at his crotch and couldn't miss the impressive bulge there. *God, this must be torture for him.* She giggled.

He frowned. "Go and get on the bed and wait for me. Eyes closed. I need a quick shower to take the edge off."

Chapter Thirteen

Makayla tugged the damask coverlet off the bed and lay down, her heart pounding in nervous anticipation. She considered putting on some sexy lingerie but rejected the idea when she thought about how much Donovan disliked his 'orders' being disregarded. Instead, she lay quietly, allowing the dulcet tones of Nina Simone to soothe and calm her.

Soon she heard the shower switch off and a couple of minutes later, she sensed Donovan in the room with her. She had her eyes closed as he had asked, but she desperately wanted to open them and see what he was doing. What was taking him so long?

"I'm just looking at you," he said quietly as if in answer to her unasked question. "Enjoying the vision of you looking beautiful and naked and laid out like a delicious banquet for me."

She sucked in a breath. God, he really had a way with words. Instantly, her nipples reacted to her growing arousal and pebbled to tight points. Moisture gathered between her thighs. She held her breath in anticipation.

"You can open your eyes now, angel." His voice was low and rough and came from directly beside her.

She allowed her lids to flutter open and stared up into his handsome face. Lust and a raw hunger emanated from his liquid brown eyes, channeling his absolute desire to her. His jaw was tight and his hard chest was dotted with spots of moisture. Jesus, he was more muscular than she'd imagined. His powerful torso looked sculpted out of stone, so carved and defined were his muscles.

The distinct V of his lower abdominals trailed underneath the towel tied low on his hips. A massive bulge jutted out between his thighs, tenting the towel and giving Makayla a very good idea of what hid beneath. Her breath stuttered and her belly churned as she trailed her gaze over every visible inch of him.

He climbed on the bed and settled his large body between her thighs so that she felt his erection brush the folds of her pussy. She moaned and tilted her hips up, wanting some friction against her aching core.

He placed his elbows tightly against her body, cupped her face in his hands then dipped his head to take her mouth in a deep, sensual kiss. He lapped at her, biting down on her lower lip before sucking it into his mouth.

She groaned and writhed beneath him. She tried to move her arms, to throw them around his neck, but she was locked securely. Pleasure swelled deep within her at his passionate conquering of her mouth, but she could only lie complacently under him and take what he was giving her. Her inability to control the kiss or to move sent a primal hunger through her. He was taking her, claiming her as his, unabashedly and ruthlessly.

He deepened the kiss, slipping his tongue between her parted lips and caressing the recesses of her mouth. She trembled uncontrollably and felt the moisture seeping in a rush from between her thighs. *Dear, God, the way he uses his mouth should be illegal.* She melted into him and matched his kiss, thrusting her hips up to rub against his rock-hard erection, trying for some relief.

He growled low in his throat and broke their connection to trail his lips across her jaw.

She panted, drawing in deep breaths. "Donovan, please," she gasped.

He ignored her, kissing a sensual trail around her neck, then down to her cleavage, all the while keeping her imprisoned beneath his powerful body. She tried to wriggle free, needing something to relieve the pleasurable ache growing low in her belly, but obviously, he wanted to torture her as he felt he'd been tortured.

Finally, he reached her breast and kissed a slow trajectory to her nipple. She held her breath then groaned loudly when his mouth closed over the taut nub and he sucked hard.

"Oh God." She arched her back the little that she could and tried to force her breast farther into his mouth.

He swirled his tongue around her nipple then bit down.

"Ahhh." The pain wasn't bad, just intense and…hot, propelling a lightning bolt of desire straight to her core.

His eyes sparkled as he looked up at her, laving the tortured peak with his tongue.

"Please, Donovan," she begged. The throbbing insistence in her belly was growing unbearable. She tried to close her legs to relieve the ache, but his body prevented any movement.

"What do you want, angel?" he asked, releasing her arms finally and sinking lower down her torso.

"I need more," she pleaded.

She watched as he settled himself between her legs and studied her sex. "What are you doing?" She gaped at him.

"Oh, baby," he breathed. "You're so wet. Your little pink folds are dripping with arousal. I have to taste you."

He dipped his head, inhaled deeply then swiped his tongue up her center.

"Oh, fuck," she groaned.

He growled into her folds, the vibrations sending sparks of pleasure shooting outward. He slipped a finger inside her and used his tongue to tease her clit, swirling it around the nub in long, languid strokes.

The sensations were tumultuous, turning her insides into a bubbling caldron of desire. She moaned and thrust her hips up, needing more friction and deeper penetration.

Donovan added another digit to the first and circled them inside her, stretching her. A twinge of pain accompanied his actions and she inhaled sharply. He pumped his fingers faster and lapped at her, sucking her clit into his mouth.

He drew his head back and watched her as he slowed the thrust of his fingers then pulled them out and massaged her clit, slowly gathering her moisture and running little circles around the sensitive nub.

She writhed under his ministrations, desperate to claim the orgasm that was hovering just out of reach. Then she felt it. Her core quivered and her insides started to tighten.

"That's it, baby," Donovan whispered. "I can feel that you're close."

Then he clamped his mouth over her sex and sucked. That was all it took to send her spiraling out of control. She cried out and stiffened as the waves of ecstasy rolled over her, leaving her trembling and weak.

She lay still, panting and trying to regain control of her erratic breathing. *Good God, I never thought it would feel like this.* Her years of awkwardly bringing herself to orgasm had not come close to preparing her for the real thing.

Donovan crawled up her body and settled himself once more between her thighs, his pelvis in line with hers so she could feel the steel hardness of his erection throbbing incessantly against her core.

Jesus, he must have some serious self-control.

He dipped his head to hers and licked her lips before taking her in a wild kiss. She was slightly taken aback by the taste of herself on him—both shocking and erotic. She opened to him and allowed him to caress her with his tongue. His kiss grew harder and more desperate until finally he pulled away and stared into her eyes.

"You. Are. So. Beautiful," he murmured. "The way you look right now, wild hair and dewy-eyed and positively satiated is so fucking hot. I think you're ready for my cock now."

She frowned. "I've been ready for that for a long time."

"No, you haven't," he disagreed. "I needed you to be soft and compliant, totally relaxed."

He slid a hand down her torso, between her breasts and over her belly until he reached her sex.

"See how wet you are?" he asked huskily. He dipped a finger in, swirling gently, and lowered his mouth to hers and spoke against her lips. "You're slick and hot and slightly swollen from your orgasm. Now, you're ready for me to fuck you."

She moaned into his mouth and rubbed her sex against his cock. He licked her lips and chuckled. "You *are* a desperate little virgin. Christ, I have to take you, and when I do, you'll be mine. Do you understand?"

She didn't really, but she was willing to agree to anything just to have him inside her finally. She bucked her hips more forcefully and whimpered.

He drew his head back to stare into her eyes. "Answer me," he demanded. "Do you understand?"

"Yes, yes," she cried. "I understand."

He smiled triumphantly and rose to his knees. She gazed at his muscular chest and arms, the muted sunlight through the drapes casting the sculpted lines of his torso in shadow, making him appear almost stone-like.

He whipped the towel from around his waist and tossed it aside. His cock bounced heavily then settled hard and erect against his lower abdomen.

She gaped at him. She'd suspected that it was big, but the actual sight of it was slightly intimidating. She gulped and looked up into his eyes.

"It's okay, angel. It'll fit," he promised. He settled once more on top of her, his arms taking his weight, dropped his head to hers and kissed her softly.

She relaxed under him and wrapped her arms around his neck, returning his kiss and moaning into his mouth.

He drew away from her. "Bring your knees up," he murmured, grasping her ankles and placing her feet flat on the mattress. He swirled his fingers over her cleft, spreading her moisture. "That's it, baby. You're so ready for me. I can't wait to feel this tight little cunt, bare, around my cock. I've never fucked anyone without a condom and the thought of your sweet little pussy fisting my shaft is sending me over the edge."

He crawled on top of her again, the head of his cock brushing over her center. He planted his elbows on either side of her head and cupped her face in both hands. Then he plunged, hard and deep.

"Arghh," she cried out as a hot pain pierced her.

She opened her eyes and stared up at the look of wild exultation crossing his features.

"Shh. Relax," he hushed her, trailing soft kisses over her face. He stilled for a moment then withdrew and plunged forward once more.

The pain receded slowly and she started to relax. She opened her legs wider and thrust up with her hips.

Donovan grunted. "That's it, baby. You feel so good. You're so fucking tight."

Spreading warmth replaced the piercing twinges and she gasped as he drilled into her harder, pulling out entirely then plunging back in to the hilt. She used her feet on the mattress as leverage and matched his rhythm, arching her back and tilting her pelvis to allow him deeper access. She pushed the residual pain to the back of her mind and focused on the building pleasure.

"Christ," he cursed. His jaw tightened as he battled with his self-control. "Keep your eyes open."

Makayla snapped her eyes open to see his hard features as he moved inside her. She dropped her gaze to his torso and watched his abdominal muscles undulating deliciously with each surge of his body.

She felt so full. He was big and rigid and so deep each thrust seemed to bump against her cervix. The sensations overwhelmed her and she groaned, the pain replaced by an intense pleasure.

He rose to his knees, scooped one hand under her back, the other under her butt, and pulled her up so she sat straddling his lap.

"Oh, my God," she choked out, the new position sending his cock surging straight to her core.

He grunted in her ear. "Yes, baby, it's fucking deep this way." He tightened his hold on her and pumped harder.

Her insides started to spasm and convulse. She whimpered as pleasure pulsated slowly outward.

"You're close," he groaned. "Come for me. Give it up, Makayla."

A dam burst and ecstasy crashed over her. "Donovan!" She went rigid in his arms, her pussy clenching and throbbing in release.

"Christ! You're fucking milking me." He grasped her tighter and held her still while he thrust his pelvis up and drilled into her harder.

She flopped against him in exhaustion and allowed him to manipulate her body to his will.

He adjusted his hold on her and clenched her hips, pulling her down while he pushed up three more times. Then he stiffened, clutching her close as he emptied inside her and roared her name.

Chapter Fourteen

Donovan stood over Makayla and gazed at her as she slept. She was lovely in slumber, her copious golden hair spread out on the pillow, her thick eyelashes fanning out on her pale cheeks.

Blood streaked her thighs and the sheet. *That'll give the maids something to talk about.* He chuckled wryly. He strode into the bathroom and filled the sink with warm water then dunked a cloth in. After returning to the bed, he swiped it over Makayla's thighs. He pulled her legs apart gently and cleaned between them, dabbing the cloth over her pink folds with care. She didn't budge. He'd obviously exhausted her. He hoped to hell that he hadn't hurt her, because there seemed to be a lot of blood, but that was to be expected, he supposed. The sight of it appealed to the darkness in his nature. He'd broken her hymen, which, he admitted, gave him a weird thrill and sent a possessiveness coursing through his veins. He didn't want to acknowledge it, but the thought of her being with any other man was abhorrent to him, a totally new and unfamiliar feeling.

He finished tending to her and climbed into bed, pulling her body tight against his and spooning her. He burrowed his head in her hair and inhaled deeply. She smelled of vanilla, shampoo and him—a heady combination. She sighed softly and nuzzled against him in her sleep, her body fitting with his perfectly.

* * * *

Donovan awoke slowly, Makayla plastered to his side, neither of them having moved much during the night. He checked the time—eight a.m. He felt great. A full night's sleep and some sensational fucking had done wonders. Beside him, Makayla yawned, stretched and opened her eyes slowly, her gazing meeting his.

"Hi there," he murmured.

"Good morning."

Her voice was huskier than usual and he hardened instantly. Shit, he had to think of something else. She'd be too sore this morning to go a second round. He shifted uncomfortably and her eyes widened when his cock brushed against her hip.

"Don't worry." He smirked. "I'm going to allow you time to recover."

She blushed and bit her bottom lip, which just made him throb harder.

"Don't do that," he groaned.

She giggled.

"Are you sore?" he asked.

She frowned and stretched. "I am bit tender," she confessed.

"Good. That means whenever you move today, you'll think of me and where I've been."

She scowled. "You *are* kinky."

"You don't know the half of it." He changed the subject. "I need to feed you. The little cheese and fruit you had last night wasn't enough."

"I am hungry," she admitted. "Do we go to one of the restaurants for breakfast?"

He gave her an incredulous look. "No, we have a butler. I'll call him and have breakfast delivered here. We'll eat on the balcony. It looks to be a lovely day."

He clambered out of bed then strode naked to the bathroom. "We'll shower together," he called over his shoulder. "I'll run the water."

Makayla stared at Donovan's retreating form, trying to grasp what she was seeing. Then the sun hit him and she gasped. His back was scarred, the lines white and ridged against his tanned skin but etched in a pattern. Two eagle's wings deliberately carved into his skin, taking up the entirety of his back. She'd never seen anything like it before. She had to ask him about it and she wanted a closer look.

She lay for a moment thinking about the events of the previous evening. One thing was certain — Donovan definitely knew what he was doing in the bedroom. She'd never dreamed that sex could be that good and seriously thought she could get hooked on the feeling. Of course, the number of women he must have experienced to put him in the sex-god league made her shudder. But he was a grown man. Of course, he would've had his fair share of women. Makayla would have had her fair share of men by this stage, too, if circumstances had allowed it. She stretched and felt a twinge deep inside and realized that she'd probably be a little tender for a while.

She got out of bed just as Donovan strode in from the bathroom. She noticed the blood streaking the formerly pristine white sheets and blushed hotly. Why hadn't she considered that? She knew why, of course — they'd both been too taken up in the moment.

Donovan gave her a scorching look. "I should have that framed," he said seriously.

Makayla gaped at him. "I suppose the next thing you're going to do is hang it from the balcony like a medieval king."

He laughed. "That's not a bad idea."

"Seriously, Donovan. It's embarrassing."

He pulled her into him and kissed the top of her head. "Don't worry about it, angel," he said with finality. "Now, shower's running. Let's go."

* * * *

They had breakfast on the balcony overlooking El Retiro. The sun blazed down on the city and the sky was crystal-clear blue. Donovan was going to some meetings and wouldn't be available to explore the city with her until later. It was a hot day so she'd spend the morning by the pool. Thinking about sightseeing around the city reminded her about Fernando's tour options and she also recalled the odd way that Donovan had acted around the manager after they'd checked in.

Intrigued, she asked, "Why did you turn so cold to Fernando yesterday?"

Donovan assessed her over the rim of his coffee mug, his mirrored aviator sunglasses making it impossible for her to read his eyes. "I didn't realize I had."

She arched an eyebrow. "You weren't, initially. It was after you introduced me."

He sighed and put his coffee mug on the table. "You're not going to like my answer."

"I'm still curious."

"Fine. It's because he was showing interest in you. In the past... On occasion, we shared women."

Makayla gasped, startled by his admission. "Do you want to share me with him?"

"Fuck, no!" he said adamantly. "That's exactly why I acted the way I did. I wanted him to know without a doubt that it would not be happening with you. Those other women were casual, one-night stands. You're mine and I don't share what's mine." He looked fierce. "I never did play well with others."

Makayla was still reeling from his pronouncement. "What did the women think of this?"

"They agreed, of course. I wouldn't force a woman to do something she wasn't comfortable with. The women I often associated with...had certain appetites. Sharing, or *ménages à trois* were just a few of those."

She needed some time to process that little nugget of information. She changed the subject. "I should have guessed you'd be fluent in Spanish," she commented, recalling him speaking with Fernando the previous evening.

"Yes. My mother made me take classes when I was younger. Back then, I hated it, but now I'm eternally grateful to her. It makes business dealings much easier. You'll find that English is not widely spoken in Madrid. Of course, there are many who speak and understand English, but in day-to-day dealings in shops and bars, smaller restaurants, et cetera? Not so much."

"Why are there so many lions in this hotel?" she asked suddenly.

He frowned. "Lions?"

"There are statues of lions in the lobby and at the front of the hotel. They seem to be popular here. Do they mean anything?"

"Do you recall me telling you that this hotel used to be a palace?"

She nodded.

"It used to belong to a nobleman and close relative of the royal family. The lions represent power. The royals incorporate lions in paintings, tapestries, statues, fountains, everywhere really, as a symbol of strength."

It made sense, she supposed. Donovan knew so much about Spain that she'd have to pick his brains. She nibbled on a croissant and formulated her next question. "I noticed your back."

He looked up from his newspaper and gazed at her impassively. "And?"

"I've never seen anything like that before."

"Does it disgust you?"

"Of course not," she said indignantly. "I guess I'm more intrigued than anything. I didn't get a very good look. I just noticed it when you turned to go into the bathroom."

He studied her for a moment, his eyes invisible behind his sunglasses. He stood suddenly and whipped off his T-shirt, his muscles bulging deliciously with the action. He turned around and spoke over his shoulder. "I wasn't hiding it from you, baby. I get mixed reactions. They're eagle's wings. Have at it. Look to your heart's content."

Makayla stepped forward and studied Donovan's back. The scarred lines raised white and stark against his olive skin in a perfect etching of two wings, the detail extraordinary. She ran her index finger over the outline of one long feather.

"It's beautiful," she whispered in awe. "Did it hurt?"

"The process is called scarification and there are various methods of achieving the end result. It did hurt, but the healing process is more uncomfortable than the actual scarification itself — at least for me. The skin is tight and itchy for some weeks afterward."

"I can't believe they wouldn't use any anesthetic to numb the area."

"It's possible to get a mild anesthetic, but the pain is part of the process, the ritual, if you like. Like a spiritual passage, using the pain to heighten the connection between mind and body. It's been used for years in a number of civilizations for various reasons."

Makayla continued to trace the outline of one wing, marveling at the detailed scar tissue. "Why the eagle's wings?" she asked.

"The eagle wings represent protection and guardianship… It appealed to that part of my nature."

"I wonder if I could bear that pain," she mused.

He spun around and took her hands in his. "No. I couldn't bear to see you go through that, and besides, I like your skin the way it is — smooth and flawless. Would you really want something like this on your body?"

She shrugged. "I've never thought about it, but no, I don't think so. I like it on you, though."

He grinned. "That's good, because it's here to stay." He looked at his watch. "Now, I need to get organized. I have a meeting in two hours."

Chapter Fifteen

Donovan finished tying his tie and looked across to where Makayla stood rummaging through a drawer. José, their butler, had unpacked for them earlier that morning while they'd been eating breakfast.

"What are you going to do while I'm in meetings?" he asked her.

"I thought I'd go to the rooftop pool." She pulled out a minuscule bikini, white with gold embellishment that would make the wearer look seven shades of fucking sinful.

"You can't wear that!" he blurted.

Startled, she looked up. "Why not?"

"Because there's barely anything to it," he snapped, snatching the top out of her hands then holding it up. "Are these two triangles supposed to cover your breasts?"

She laughed. "It was your personal shopper who purchased it."

"Don't you have a one piece you can wear?"

She shook her head. "No, it seems that she just included bikinis. Stop being a prude."

He supposed he was being a little prudish, but the thought of her alone at the pool wearing that sexy little number didn't sit well with him. But he would have to deal with it and stop acting like a jealous asshole.

"Fine," he conceded. "But please be careful."

"Of course," she agreed, standing on tiptoe to plant a kiss on his mouth.

He gripped her around the waist and took the kiss deeper, slipping his tongue between her lips to tangle with hers. He pulled away. "Think of me when you're sore today."

She rolled her eyes and nodded.

Donovan grabbed his briefcase and left the suite. He wanted to pass by Fernando on the way out and tell him that Makayla was off limits. He found him in his office. He knocked once then entered, taking a seat opposite him.

"Donovan." Fernando nodded.

"Fernando." Donovan nodded back.

"To what do I owe this visit? Is everything to your liking in the suite?"

"Everything is in order, as usual."

"And how is the lovely Makayla this morning?"

"She's fine. She's the reason I wanted to see you, actually. To emphasize to you that she's off limits."

Fernando smirked. "Yes, your possessive attitude when you arrived told me that she's special to you. Pity, she's very beautiful." He assessed Donovan thoughtfully. "There's something about her. She seems innocent. Not your usual type."

"No, she's not my usual type," Donovan agreed. "That's one of the reasons that I won't be sharing her, even if she wasn't opposed to the idea."

"Will you be taking her to Infierno?"

"No. She's different. I don't want to tarnish her purity with that lifestyle. She's not aware of that aspect of my life and I want it to stay that way, so please don't mention anything."

"Of course. You can rely on my discretion." He tilted his head. "This is very unlike you, Donovan."

Donovan shrugged. "What can I say? She's special and I'll do anything to protect my relationship with her. I'm also worried about her getting around the city unaccompanied. Can you recommend a good GPS application that we can download to our phones? I'd like to be able to assist her if she were to become lost."

"I know of a decent one. I'll text you the information."

Donovan stood and nodded his thanks. "I'll see you later."

* * * *

Makayla had slathered herself in sunscreen and wore a large floppy hat. She sat on the steps of the pool, waist deep in the water. The rooftop was busy, the hot weather keeping many by the pool instead of exploring the city. She stood then sauntered over to her sun lounger, suddenly feeling sleepy, no doubt from a little jet lag.

She settled herself on the lounger and took a sip of the juice she'd ordered from the bar. Before he'd left that morning, Donovan had told her to put anything she purchased on the room tab. She felt a little guilty, but she wasn't splurging, even though she sensed that that's exactly what Donovan wanted her to do. She'd ordered a sandwich and a tropical juice for lunch. She hoped that they could go to the piano bar in the lobby that evening. She wanted to try *cava*, Spain's version of champagne, and some of the traditional *tapas*.

She looked up to see an attractive Spanish man leaning over her. She assumed he was Spanish due to his Mediterranean coloring. His sun-burnished, olive skin and thick head of black hair singled him out as such.

"Miss Carrington?"

"Yes," she responded.

He held his hand out to her. "I'm Gabriel Sosa. I'm the Quality Assurance Director for Totally Five Star Hotels."

She shook his hand warmly. "It's a pleasure to meet you."

"*Encantado.*" He raised her hand to his lips and kissed it.

"I noticed that Mr. King was staying with us again and I wanted to introduce myself to his lovely lady friend." He motioned to her sun lounger. "May I sit?"

"Of course." She smiled.

He settled himself on her long, wide sunbed.

His white polo shirt emphasized his golden tan and his shorts covered firm, muscular thighs. He was an attractive man.

"Do you live here?" she asked him.

"No, I live in London, but I'm from Madrid. I travel a lot for work and try to get here as much as possible." He smiled. "Particularly in the summers."

* * * *

Donovan had checked their suite—no Makayla. She must still be at the pool. He tugged off his tie then went in search of her. She'd mentioned the rooftop pool, so he'd start there. He stepped off the elevator and scanned the pool area. He saw her immediately, dressed in that minuscule excuse for a bikini, her breasts barely contained. A floppy hat adorned her head and large, round sunglasses hid her eyes. She was a vision, gorgeous and sexy, and being slobbered over by Gabriel Sosa. *What the fuck?* He couldn't believe that the man had planted himself on her lounger, as if he belonged there. Donovan strode angrily toward the pair. Sosa's eyes were hidden behind mirrored sunglasses but Donovan knew his gaze would be riveted on Makayla's breasts. He drew level with them and glared down.

"Ah, Mr. King," Sosa greeted. "I was just introducing myself to your lovely lady friend."

"Obviously," Donovan drawled sarcastically.

"Gabriel was just telling me what to visit while I'm here," Makayla said, seemingly unaware of Donovan's irritation.

"Thank you, Sosa," he said, his tone icy.

Sosa obviously got the message. Quickly, he rose to his feet. "It was a pleasure, Makayla. Please don't hesitate to contact me if you need anything." He nodded to Donovan. "Mr. King."

Donovan watched him saunter away, stopping now and again to greet guests.

He looked down at Makayla. She was spreading sunscreen on her arms and looking for all the world like she hadn't noticed his jealousy.

"Let me help," he said shortly.

He scooped her up, depositing her farther down the sunbed, and sat behind her. He squeezed some cream onto his hands and started massaging her shoulders, then he ran his hands down over her cleavage, slipping his fingers under her bikini top and just missing her nipples.

She shuddered beneath him and he felt himself grow solid. He leaned down to speak into her ear. "You look so hot. You know that man, Gabriel Sosa, was hitting on you, right?"

She gave him an exasperated look over her shoulder. "He was just being friendly, Donovan."

"If he hadn't hit on you yet, he would have eventually," he said. "I know what he's like. He can never pass up a beautiful woman."

"Well, I definitely wouldn't have taken him up on his offer," she said.

"You're right. You would definitely *not* have taken him up on it," he agreed with feeling.

She sighed. "Why don't you change into your board shorts and join me? I'm going for a swim." She stood and took her sunglasses and hat off then strode over to the pool.

Fuck, those bikini bottoms barely covered her pert little ass. Her backside swayed enticingly as she walked. He noticed the men nearby all stopped what they were doing to stare at her, and she was oblivious to the attention she was receiving. He gazed around the pool and thought that there seemed to be a lot of men around.

She reached the steps and delicately walked into the water. He should go back to the suite and change into his board shorts, but he wanted to watch Makayla a bit longer. She swam some laps then climbed gracefully out of the pool.

Donovan was staring at her and not believing his eyes. Her white bikini had basically turned transparent—fuck! He shot to his feet and grabbed her towel. One prick of a guy was actually drooling, his mouth open as he blatantly eye-fucked her.

He stormed toward her and threw the towel around her body. He shot a threatening glare at the slobbering guy. "Keep your eyes to yourself, asshole!"

"Donovan, what are you doing?" Makayla asked in dismay.

"Your bikini is see-through when it's wet," he grated between clenched teeth. He had to settle down. It wasn't her fault. But he'd certainly fire the idiot personal shopper.

"What?" she gasped in horror. "I didn't know."

"Did you not notice that the ratio of men to women suddenly grew? They're all here to stare at you."

He started packing up her things and shoving them into her beach bag. "We're going. I think you've provided these assholes with enough of a show."

He glanced at her and noticed too late the trembling of her mouth. Shit, he was acting like an ass. "Come here," he said gruffly, grabbing her hand then pulling her toward him. "I'm sorry." He wrapped his arms around her and held her close. "I'm being a bastard. I know it's not your fault. I'm just furious knowing all these pricks are ogling you and seeing a lot more than they should."

She sniffled against his chest. He'd upset her and he felt like a real shit. She'd feel mortified and embarrassed enough without him adding to her self-consciousness. "Let's go up to the room. We'll have a rest before we head out," he said quietly.

Chapter Sixteen

The next few days flew by for Makayla. They explored Madrid between Donovan's meetings. They strolled through the Prado, took a tour of the Palacio Real de Madrid and watched the Changing of the Guard. The guide at the palace explained that the royal family no longer lived there, only using it for state ceremonies. They took morning walks through the park and shopped along the Gran Vía and Calle Serrano. She was eating more than usual as she found that all the activity gave her an appetite, although she hadn't gotten used to the Spanish mealtimes — they ate breakfast up until one p.m., lunch between two thirty and three thirty, and dinner wasn't served until around nine p.m. One particular night, Donovan had left her for the evening, explaining that he was meeting a business associate. He hadn't returned to their suite until three in the morning but she had assumed it was the late hours that the Spanish kept.

She'd called her mother a couple of times and had been relieved to find that she was doing very well and even enjoying her stay at the treatment facility.

Knowing that her mother was getting the care and therapy that she so desperately needed was a load off Makayla's mind. It meant that Makayla could relax and enjoy her time away.

She was checking her email when Donovan strolled into the sitting room from the balcony where he'd been taking a phone call. He looked so handsome and tanned from their time in the sun. He'd rolled his white shirt up to the elbows, looking laid-back and casual in his dark tan chinos and dress shoes. His hair curled at his collar, an unruly wave flopping on his forehead with the five o'clock shadow on his jaw giving him a hard, masculine edge. His collar was open, revealing a triangle of firm, tanned flesh, lightly sprinkled with hair. He really was edible and, at times like this, she found it hard to believe that he was with her. She stared at Donovan, drinking him in.

He smirked at her. "Enjoying the view?"

She giggled and blushed at being caught ogling him so blatantly.

"Come here," he ordered, his voice thick.

Butterflies started in her stomach as she stood and walked slowly toward him.

"On your knees."

She licked her lips, knelt and stared up at him, waiting for his next command.

He undid his zipper and pulled out his erect, thick cock, the bulbous crown beading with moisture.

"Have you ever given head, angel?"

"No," she whispered. She was anxious to taste him, to lick the pre-cum from his tip.

"Good. Let's have a lesson." His voice was like gravel. "Take me in your mouth, baby."

She leaned forward and grasped the base of him then closed her lips around the head.

He groaned and jutted forward a little with his hips. "That's it, take me deeper."

She licked the tip, and he shuddered. Taking him farther into her mouth then sucking hard, she swirled her tongue along his length.

He growled a curse and pushed forward, grasping a handful of her hair in his fist and using it to manipulate her head.

She sank lower on him, sucking and licking, relishing the musky taste of him. He pushed her head down and thrust in and out of her mouth until she felt his tip hit the back of her throat.

"Fuck, baby," he groaned. "Relax your jaw."

She fought back a choke and did what he asked. He swelled in her mouth and his rigid length bumped against the back of her throat as he propelled himself in and out.

He slid between her lips and she pumped the base of his cock. She looked up at him from beneath lowered lashes at his jaw, tight with the effort of maintaining his control. He stared down at her with such intensity, she felt like he could look into her soul.

She pumped and sucked harder, her lips wide at the thick root of him. Her saliva made his glide between her lips smooth and slick.

"I'm going to come," he grated between clenched teeth. "I want you to swallow, but I'll understand if you don't want to." He gasped the last, his control obviously about to snap. She hastened her movements and pumped her fist at the base of his cock, telling him with her actions that she wanted to taste him.

He thrust forward, tightening his fist in her hair, then with a roar, he came hard, lodging his cock in the back of her throat and spilling into her.

He stood for a moment, immobile, his shaft still in her mouth and his fist entwined in her hair. Then he let go of her and removed himself from her mouth before helping her to her feet and kissing her passionately. "Are you okay?" he asked against her lips.

"I'm better than okay," she murmured. "I enjoyed that"

She felt his mouth curl into a smile "That was perfect, baby. You give good head."

Makayla pulled back and grinned happily, feeling warm and slightly giddy at his praise.

Donovan looked at his watch. "We're going to be late. I'll go up to the restaurant. You finish getting ready and meet me there."

* * * *

Donovan finished texting one of his club managers back in Australia. It was difficult with the time difference to keep updated, so they tended to email and text rather than speak on the phone.

He knew the moment Makayla walked into the restaurant. The air seemed to shift and he physically felt her presence. The table he'd asked for was at the opposite end of the room. He looked up and watched her start in his direction. He froze. Her low-cut jersey dress had a neckline so severe that it nearly reached her navel. Obviously, she was unable to wear a bra, and her nipples poked against the soft fabric. She'd filled out a little since she'd been away with him. Her hips were rounded nicely and her breasts were fuller—she was a walking wet dream. As he watched her progress, he noticed something else—people had actually stopped eating and talking and were staring at her. He realized with a jolt that he'd advertised to the entire fucking restaurant that she'd just given him head. Her lips were puffy and swollen from where he'd fucked her mouth, and the back of her hair, obviously unnoticed by her, was mussed from where he'd gripped it in his fist. He glanced around at the other diners and saw the men undressing her with their eyes as her delectable hips and plump, lush breasts swayed provocatively.

He shot up from his chair, the legs scraping backward loudly, and tore over to her. She smiled then frowned when she saw his face. He grasped her arm and tugged her with him in the opposite direction.

"Donovan, what are you doing?" she asked in alarm.

He'd caught sight of the back of the dress when she'd turned. The dress ended so low on her back that he could just make out the top of her ass crease. *Fuck me, that personal shopper has a lot to answer for.*

"Is everything all right, sir?" the maître d' asked with a frown.

"Fine," he said over his shoulder. "We've decided to eat in our suite."

He called for the elevator, tugged Makayla in behind him, then pushed her against the wall.

He was turned on and furious at the same time. He hated men looking at her as if they wanted to fuck her, but knowing that they coveted what was his was hot. Seeing her stop a restaurant dead in its tracks excited him, but knowing that every man in there would recognize that she'd just sucked him off had him feeling positively murderous.

He had to have her immediately, had to mark her, claim her as his. He dragged her dress up. Fuck, she wasn't wearing underwear. "No panties," he groaned against her ear.

"I couldn't with this dress," she panted. "The back's too low."

He growled in her ear and slipped a finger inside her tight, slick channel. She was always so *ready* for him—it drove him wild. "You're so wet for me, baby."

He cupped her ass and lifted her. "Wrap your legs around my waist," he ordered, his voice thick with desperation.

She complied quickly and he pushed her back against the wall then fumbled with his chinos to release his aching cock. "You have to tell me if you're too sore."

She shook her head and clenched her legs around him tighter.

He drew back, lined himself up with her sex, and thrust deeply. They groaned in unison, her tight cunt gripping his cock like a fist. He pulled back and pumped in again, pushing her back up the side of the elevator with his powerful drives. He grunted like an animal each time he plunged into her. She threw her head back and held onto his shoulders. He rutted frantically, fucking her like a wild beast. He couldn't help himself. He was crazed with desire and the need to possess her.

He felt the lift glide to a halt and he slammed his fist on the stop button.

She gasped and moaned, rolling her head from side to side.

His cock swelled bigger still, his balls tightening with lust.

"Why no bra, Makayla?" he asked in her ear on a powerful thrust. "You know every fucker in that restaurant was staring at your tight little nipples." He released a hand from her backside and massaged a breast roughly, pinching the nipple hard.

She moaned and he dipped his mouth to hers to swallow the sound, shoving his tongue between her lips forcefully.

She broke away from their kiss. "I couldn't with this dress."

"That. Fucking. Dress. Should. Be. Illegal." He punctuated each word with a fierce drive of his hips.

Her insides started to quiver and pulse. She was close. He dropped his hand between them to find her clit, pressing the little bundle of nerves then biting the tendon that connected her throat and shoulder.

She cried out and shuddered in his arms, her slick little channel throbbing around his stiff cock, milking his release from him. He pumped twice more then came hard, groaning low in his throat as he spilled his seed into her.

Chapter Seventeen

Donovan left her alone again, like the previous two nights—he'd been leaving their hotel for a couple of hours. When he returned, he was exhausted and fell into bed with barely a grunt of acknowledgment for her.

He'd just left, telling her once more that he'd be gone for two hours, running errands—she didn't believe him.

She stared at his laptop, which he'd left open and logged in. She bit her lip, debating with herself. Finally, she threw caution aside and approached the computer. She opened his email and scrolled through, noting a lot of business correspondence, a couple of emails from his father and a few from people she assumed were friends.

Next, she checked the history, something catching her immediate attention—a website dedicated to BDSM. She clicked on it, unsure what to expect, but what popped up on the screen sent her pulse into overdrive.

A gorgeous woman, lithe and long-legged, dressed in a black latex corset tied so tightly that her breasts spilled out of the top. Her mask was black leather to match her gag, her hands were tied above her head and attached to a chain. She had some sort of bar between her legs, spreading them impossibly wide.

A muscular man stood behind her, chest bare, powerful legs clothed in black leather, a vicious-looking whip in his hand.

Makayla's insides tightened and fluttered as she gazed at the image, desire coiling through her to pool between her thighs. She was aroused, she realized with a start. She clicked through more images of women and men being dominated. In one, a woman knelt in front of a man, her head bowed in supplication, her hands cuffed behind her. She wasn't gagged, just blindfolded. The man held a cat-o'-nine-tails and was brushing the leather fronds across her flesh. The next image showed him bringing the whip down on her back, making her arch, her mouth open wide and her nipples pebbled hard and hugely erect. In fact, she had the most prominent nipples Makayla had ever seen, like pencil erasers. She shifted in her seat and squeezed her legs together, trying to give some relief to her aching core. She wanted to do this. She wanted to pass control to someone else, to put complete power in their hands to use her as they wished. It was an odd desire, she realized, and she wasn't quite sure where it stemmed from. She would guess from the fact that she had been in control for so long. That she'd held the reins, trying to keep her and her mother together and safe. She'd had to be strong and make the decisions. This lifestyle turned that around. Here, she wouldn't have to make choices. She'd just have to submit and succumb. She also had to concede that the little pain that Donovan had inflicted on her, she'd enjoyed. He hadn't done anything serious, just pinching her nipples and a bite to her neck — but she'd liked it.

She stayed at his laptop, reading as much as she could, intrigued and aroused. Looking at dozens of photos of whips, nipple clamps, vibrators, handcuffs and a number of items that she was totally unfamiliar with. Was Donovan into this lifestyle? Had he ever done these things? She couldn't be sure. Perhaps the website had just popped up onto the screen accidently when he'd been searching for something else. Although there was no doubt that he had a dominant personality, he ordered her around in the bedroom *and* out of it, she complied willingly and without question, enjoying his domineering possessiveness.

All the reading and images had made her desperately stimulated. She closed all the tabs and left the laptop as she'd found it. She switched the iPod dock on, choosing Massive Attack's *Mezzanine* album, and climbed into bed.

Makayla lay in the cool, soft sheets, thinking about what she'd learned. She cupped her breast and squeezed hard, pinching her nipple roughly. Moaning and smoothing her other hand down her torso and delving two fingers into her slick folds. She thrust her hips up, pushing her fingers in deeper and adding a third, licking her lips and increasing the pressure on her nipple, a groan erupting from deep in her throat. Pressing her thumb against her clit, she shuddered, her breathing growing choppy and erratic.

* * * *

Donovan made his way to their suite. He looked at his watch to find that it was just after midnight and, no doubt, Makayla would be curled up in bed fast asleep. He swore softly under his breath. He really needed a release. The evening had done nothing but amp up his arousal and he wanted to fuck—hard.

He sighed and slipped his security card into the door mechanism then pushed it open quietly. Inside, he recognized Massive Attack playing. Perhaps she wasn't asleep after all.

He strode into the bedroom, removing his shirt, and stopped dead on the threshold.

Makayla lay in bed all right, but she wasn't asleep. A deep flush hued her cheeks, little whimpers erupting from her. The sheet had dropped down to her waist and she was cupping one plump breast and squeezing, her other hand hidden under the sheet, but he could tell it was buried in her pussy. Her legs were spread wide, tenting the covers as she thrust her hips up.

She hadn't heard him enter, the music and her moans drowning out any noise he may have made.

He stared, mesmerized for a moment by the sensual vision she made. He frowned as he remembered his order not to touch herself. Granted, he'd given that instruction back in Australia and hadn't had cause to issue it since, but still, he had to admit that watching her masturbate was both erotic and infuriating. Infuriating because *he* wanted to be the one to give her pleasure—taking it from someone else, even from herself, seemed to be a betrayal. He knew it was stupid, but those were his feelings. Everything that revolved around this angel had him in conflict and acting like a complete moron.

He moved closer to the bed. Her moans were growing louder, her breathing choppier, indicating that she was near to completion. She wouldn't be given the opportunity to bring herself off, however. He'd finish what she'd started.

"What are you doing, angel?" he purred.

She gasped, snapping her violet eyes open in wild confusion, her blush deepening and spreading over her features.

"D-Donovan, you scared the life out of me. I didn't hear you come in." She scrambled to pull the sheet up to her chin.

He whipped the covers off her and flung them aside. She squeezed her legs together.

"No, no, no," he murmured, climbing onto the bed and pulling her thighs apart so he could crawl between them. "My turn. By the way, did I say that you could touch yourself?"

She shook her head and wouldn't meet his eyes, her lush bottom lip caught between her teeth. He studied her pussy, moist, pink and swollen from her arousal. Her neat golden curls glistened with her moisture.

"You've been a bad girl," he whispered, dipping his head lower to inhale her. She smelled so fucking good, tangy and sexual. "Were you close, baby? Were you just about to come?"

She didn't answer him. He looked up her body. He fucking loved that he could still embarrass her. She was still so sweet and shy.

"Answer me," he demanded.

"Yes," she said so softly that he barely heard her.

"Well, I got home just in time, didn't I?"

He flattened his tongue and licked up her swollen center. She groaned and jerked. He grasped her hips to keep her still.

"Got home just in time to make you come, because *I* want to take you there. *I* want to give that pleasure to you." He spoke into her wet folds, enjoying the way she writhed beneath him in frustration.

"Please," she begged. "Why are you torturing me?"

He blew softly on her pussy then closed his mouth over her and sucked hard.

"Argh." She thrust her hips up and ground her pelvis against his mouth.

He sucked harder, driving his tongue into her cunt and swirling it around. She was so wet and so swollen that he knew she'd come hard and fast.

He slipped two fingers inside her and massaged the front wall of her passage. She shuddered and spread her thighs wide, gyrating against his hand. He thrust deeper and rubbed harder.

"How many fingers did you use on yourself, baby? How many did you slip inside this tight, wet pussy?" His voice was rough with his own desire and need for release, but he maintained control. He wanted to get her off like this first.

"Three," she gasped brokenly.

Fuck! He slipped another finger inside her and felt the stretch of her channel, her arousal making his glide slick and swift. He clamped his mouth on her clit and sucked, then he felt the convulsions of her internal muscles signaling her release. She whimpered and stiffened, clamping down on his fingers as the orgasm tore through her. He lapped at her gently, bringing her down through her climax.

He couldn't wait any longer. His cock was throbbing so hard he was literally aching.

He urged her up the bed. She was limp and languid, her eyelids heavy. He flipped her onto her stomach and pushed her knees up.

"Grab onto the headboard," he ordered. "And don't let go."

He waited until she'd unsteadily gripped the wood board then he lined his cock up with her entrance. He clutched her hips and drove into her—hard—propelling himself balls deep on a roar. "Fuck!"

He bottomed out in her, stretching her wide, her swollen pussy gripping him tightly.

She whimpered and thrust her ass back against his pelvis. Using her hips he manipulated her body, pushing her forward and yanking her back onto his aching length, driving into her forcefully, his balls slapping against her clit.

He bent over her back and clamped his teeth onto the soft flesh between her neck and shoulder, nipping and sucking. She shuddered and groaned his name, knuckles white where she gripped the headboard.

She was like his own personal fuck doll. He knew he was a bastard for thinking of her in such a way, but he couldn't help it. She was so petite and compliant that he could literally fling her around, manipulating her body with ease to satiate his base needs. And she was so fucking responsive. He hardly had to work at all before she was coming for him.

He fucked her harder, setting a punishing rhythm and drilling into her soft body like his life depended on it.

"Come, Makayla," he shouted, his own release bearing down on him like a freight train.

She moaned and pushed back, and he felt her climax hit her, her muscles contracting around his cock.

He barked a curse, words failing him as he pumped once more, gripping her hips and circling his pelvis, drawing out his orgasm as he released his pent-up frustration.

Chapter Eighteen

"I should be more careful with you," Donovan murmured.

Makayla looked down to where Donovan was stroking her hip and noticed the fingermarks, pale purple imprints on her skin. She shrugged. "It doesn't hurt."

"Still. I obviously grasped you too hard. I was a little crazed last night."

Yes, he had been a little wild. Was it because he'd walked in on her pleasuring herself? God, she blushed just thinking about it. Or was it something else that had made him like that?

"I'm going to the gym," he announced, diving out of bed. He headed to the walk-in wardrobe. "It's been a few days since I've worked out."

Makayla thought she might join him. Some exercise would do her good.

She followed Donovan into the wardrobe and bent over to rummage through a chest of drawers for a yoga outfit.

She felt him behind her, his hard length rubbing the crevice of her ass.

"You shouldn't do that, baby," he said huskily. "You bent over naked does things to me."

She stilled, allowing him to work himself over her backside. He grasped her hips gently while he massaged her butt cheeks with his cock and groaned.

"Aren't we going to the gym, Romeo?" she murmured.

"Yes." He slapped her ass. "Put some clothes on so I'm not distracted."

She giggled. Minutes later, she was dressed in little yoga shorts and a tight sports top, her thick hair in a high ponytail.

She wandered out into the sitting room where Donovan sat watching the morning news. He stood and stared at her.

"That outfit is fucking distracting, Makayla," he stated, looking her up and down.

"It's workout gear. What do you want me to wear to the gym?"

He sighed. "If any fucker looks at you funny, I won't be responsible for my actions."

She rolled her eyes at him. "Come on, you possessive weirdo."

* * * *

They worked out for an hour and a half. Makayla positively drooled over Donovan on the treadmill. He wore a tank top that displayed his tanned, muscular arms to perfection. Makayla wasn't the only one drooling. Two women working out together were casting longing looks in his direction, bending down in front of him and trying everything in their power to get his attention. For his part, Donovan ignored them.

It warmed her to realize that he was so impervious to the flirting women.

An hour later, however, a young man wandered up to Makayla and struck up a conversation. He was an American visiting Madrid for work and wanted to know if she was interested in sightseeing with him. He obviously didn't realize that she was with someone. From the treadmill, Donovan shot daggers in their direction. Makayla declined politely, trying desperately to discourage him without offense. She wanted him to leave her alone before Donovan abandoned the running machine for some different physical activity. Finally, the guy got the message and wandered over to the weight machine, leaving Makayla to finish her yoga stretches in peace.

Donovan immediately finished on the treadmill and walked over to her, rubbing his face and body down with a towel. When he reached her, he grasped her under the arms and hauled her up from the floor. He looked pointedly in the direction of the young man who was now studying them curiously. Then he bent his head to hers and took her mouth in a deep, drugging kiss, grasping her ass cheeks, pulling her into him and rubbing his erection against her shamelessly. He smelled of spicy male sweat—sexy and masculine. She knew what he was doing. He was marking his territory like a caveman, but she didn't try to stop him, realizing that he needed to do that with her.

He drew away then kissed her forehead before projecting another glare at the poor guy across the gym.

"I think you've made your point," she said quietly.

He gave her an impassive look. "Do you? I'm not sure. Perhaps those yoga moves you were doing give men the wrong impression," he said curtly.

She yanked herself out of his arms and bent to collect her towel and water bottle from the floor. "That was unfair," she said, her voice cold. She turned and headed for the door.

She heard him curse then felt him behind her.

"I'm sorry." He grasped her elbow to halt her. "That was uncalled for." He sighed. "I don't know what comes over me where you're concerned. I have this desperate need to protect you."

"I don't require protection from *everyone*," she said in exasperation.

He grinned sheepishly. "Point taken. Now, let's shower and hit the streets for some more sightseeing."

Chapter Nineteen

They'd had a fabulous day walking around the city,
sightseeing and eating ice cream in the park. Donovan
had no meetings, so they had the entire day to
themselves. Now they sat relaxing in the lobby of the
Totally Five Star, listening to live piano music and
drinking *cava*.

Makayla wore a black halter neck dress in a soft silk
fabric and she loved it. It made her feel sophisticated
and sexy. It wasn't short, falling to just above her
knees, but it was fitted and showed off her new curves
to their best advantage. Donovan had grumbled about
it, of course, mumbling something about firing the
personal shopper, but he hadn't tried to stop her from
wearing it. She had to confess that she quite liked the
admiring glances that were being thrown her way. She
wasn't used to being on the receiving end of
appreciative male attention, but she'd changed since
she'd met Donovan—she recognized that. She was
more confident and more self-assured. She didn't
fidget so much and she held herself with poise. Also,
she only wore her glasses for reading now. Before,

she'd worn them to hide behind, preferring to blend into the background and direct attention away from herself.

Donovan, predictably, had placed a possessive hand at her back as he'd guided her through the hotel lobby.

A waiter placed a plate of *tapas* on their table, small squares of tortilla bread with tomato and cheese and bite-sized *croquetas*. She took a *croqueta* and bit into the deep-fried morsel. It was filled with a thick cheese sauce and Spanish *jamón*. Flavor burst on her tongue.

Donovan took a square of tortilla. "You know, the word *tapas* originates from the verb *tapar*, which means to cover. There are several explanations about how the *tapa* came about. Some say it was originally a piece of bread used to cover the sherry glass and protect it from flies. Others say that King Felipe III passed a law that all alcoholic beverages must be consumed with food to prevent drunken, bawdy behavior. The bartender had to place a cover of food or bread on top of the glass as part of the purchase. There are other theories, of course, but my mother told me that the Felipe III law was the correct explanation." He shrugged. "I think it also depends on what part of Spain you come from as to the preferred account."

"I think it's a fabulous idea. To have little portions of food to accompany a drink. It makes sense," Makayla responded, taking a piece of bread and tomato. "Also, they eat so late here that everyone would be starving by dinner time without *tapas* to tide them over."

"Yes, there is that. The Spanish do keep very late hours," he agreed. Donovan studied her, his gaze lowering to her chest, his lips compressed into a thin line. "Are you cold, angel?"

"The air conditioning is a little chilly," she admitted. "Why?"

He leaned toward her. "Your hard little nipples are visible under your dress."

"Oh," she breathed. That was one of the problems with going braless. She was just about to reach for her pashmina when Fernando appeared at their table.

"Mr. King, Miss Carrington." He nodded and took Makayla's hand in his. "I hope you're enjoying your stay with us."

She smiled. "Very much so. Thank you."

He kept hold of her hand, running circles over the back of it with his thumb. His gaze dropped to her chest and he licked his lips, his pupils dilating. Donovan stiffened beside her then yanked her hand out of Fernando's hold and dragged her chair alongside his own.

"We've discussed this, Fernando," he said, his voice ominously low.

The man smiled. "Of course. I shall leave you to enjoy your night." He looked at Donovan with a raised eyebrow. "Will I be seeing you later?"

Donovan cursed quietly and threw him a threatening glare. Fernando merely chuckled.

"Good evening." He nodded briefly and disappeared between the tables.

"Why would you see him later?" Makayla enquired curiously.

"No reason," Donovan said curtly and looked at his watch. "Let's go back to the suite."

His tone didn't brook disagreement, so she finished her drink in silence and followed him back to their rooms.

* * * *

Makayla flicked through the Canal+ channels trying to find something interesting in English to watch. She surreptitiously observed Donovan. He seemed restless and hadn't settled down since they'd returned to their suite. She'd made up her mind that if he left again that evening, she was going to follow him. It would be a little difficult, getting out of the suite undetected, but the fact that he wouldn't be expecting to be followed would be on her side. It meant that he wouldn't be looking out for her. She'd changed into flats in readiness and hoped fervently that wherever he planned to go, he would go on foot. She didn't know how to say 'follow that cab' in Spanish.

Donovan walked into the bedroom and emerged a couple of minutes later, texting. He had a small bag with him.

"I have to go out for a while, baby. I'm sorry." He walked toward her then kissed her, plunging his tongue into her mouth and slanting his lips across hers. He grabbed her ass and massaged the cheeks hard, grinding his pelvis into her. "I won't be long," he promised.

Makayla forced herself to wait until she knew that Donovan would be in the elevator. Then she raced out after him, punching the button for the service lift. She tapped her foot impatiently until the lift reached the lobby. She stepped out cautiously and was relieved to see Donovan striding toward the lobby doors. She followed him, keeping at a safe distance. She needn't have worried, however, since he was striding with singular purpose, paying no attention to anything around him and definitely not bothering to look behind himself. The street signs indicated that he was heading in the direction of Chueca. Not unusual.

Chueca had many bars and clubs. If he *was* actually meeting for business, it wouldn't be an odd place to convene, particularly given that Donovan's associates were mostly in the same line of work—clubs.

She kept a discreet distance and eventually they emerged in Chueca, the narrow streets, robust nightlife and fetish shops signifying the barrio's specialty.

Donovan stopped outside a nondescript entranceway, checked his watch then opened the door and stepped through.

Makayla crept closer, keeping flush against the wall and waiting a few minutes until she was confident that Donovan wouldn't be coming back out any time soon. She walked away from the wall and stared up at an unremarkable sign above the entrance. It was odd in its lack of showiness—*Infierno*, lettered in simple red cursive.

"Infierno," she whispered. "Hell."

Makayla paced outside the entrance for some minutes, working up the courage to go in. She wasn't sure what to expect and it scared the life out of her. She gave herself a mental pep talk then strode with purpose through the door.

The dim interior was ominous, and it took a moment for her eyes to adjust. There was a heavy beat of music coming from somewhere within the bowels of the building. A stairwell led directly down to another level. She walked gingerly down the steps and over to a young man standing guard behind a desk. He wore black leather pants and what looked like a spiked dog collar around his neck. His lean bare chest was tanned and oiled and his short, dark hair gelled into severe points.

He looked her up and down approvingly, his gaze settling on her breasts. She shifted uncomfortably and cleared her throat.

He collected himself and met her eyes. *"¿Puedo ayudarle? Este club es solo para los miembros,"* he said in rapid Spanish.

Makayla wrung her hands in confusion, suddenly feeling out of her depth, her gaze alighting on a thick black curtain directly behind the man. Was he telling her that she couldn't enter?

He looked her up and down again. *"¿Habla ingles?"*

She understood enough to recognize that question. "Yes," she said, relief coloring her voice.

"Can I help you?" He spoke in hesitant, heavily accented English. "This club is members only."

"Oh, I was looking for someone." She said slowly and clearly. "Donovan King."

The man arched his eyebrows in surprise. *"El Rey?"*

Makayla frowned in confusion.

"The King," he elaborated. "The King of Infierno."

Chapter Twenty

Makayla froze, mouth agape in dismay. What the hell was this club? But she didn't have to stretch her imagination far. Her discovery on Donovan's laptop, the oddly attired 'doorman' and the preferential entry requirements pointed squarely in one direction — this was a BDSM club. A BDSM club that Donovan was obviously highly placed in, if his 'The King' moniker was anything to go by.

She tried to calm her beating heart and get a grip on her emotions. The young man behind the counter was studying her curiously, obviously wondering what her relationship was to Donovan. Though what *exactly* she was to Donovan had yet to be established. The term girlfriend hadn't even been tossed around in passing, just his constant references to her as his. It wasn't lost on her that she hadn't claimed that privilege for him. They hadn't even discussed exclusivity, and thinking about that now gave her a sick feeling.

"Are you his girlfriend?" The man finally asked the question that she'd just been contemplating.

"Something like that," she murmured, settling for a suitably vague response.

"Any friend of The King's is welcome here," he said amiably in his sexy accent. "We will find out soon enough if he does not know you."

She understood from her brief investigative foray into BDSM that it didn't always entail sex. Often it didn't involve any sex at all, but was all about the control and submission aspect. At least she could hope that Donovan wasn't on the other side of that curtain fucking some beautiful woman's brains out. They obviously had a bar here, so perhaps he was just catching up with friends.

She breathed deeply, squared her shoulders and prepared to face what was on the inside of Infierno.

The young man swept the curtain aside and motioned her forward.

She wandered into a bar area, the music louder and clearer inside. It was a rhythm that pulsed and beat with a heavy bass, something she didn't recognize. People around the bar reclined in lounge chairs or perched on stools. They had one thing in common—they were all dressed in similar fashion—namely PVC, latex, leather—and were very skimpily clad. It was a kinky, fetish sex bar—not that she'd ever been to one—but she imagined this would be an excellent example. She stood on the threshold, keeping to the shadows, taking it all in. Nearby, a woman knelt by the feet of a man who was chatting to a gentleman next to him and patting the woman's head, stroking her hair while she remained silently stoic in head-bowed submission.

A woman dressed in a corset and impossibly high stilettos strolled past. She held a leash attached to a collar around a man's neck. He walked behind her sedately, head down and clothed in nothing save for a pair of black leather briefs that left little to the imagination.

Cries and moans echoed in the large space, emanating from different corners. Men and women alike were strapped to various contraptions and looked to be involved in what she now understood to be scenes. Dominants wielded bondage apparatus, whips, paddles and numerous toys, the music providing a sinister background to the kinky activities.

Makayla was at once shocked and intrigued. It was one thing to read about these things, another to see them first-hand. To watch a person wielding a whip and lashing the flesh of another—it was alarming stuff.

She assessed the scenes from her vantage point in the background for a few minutes longer, absorbing the atmosphere and willing her heart to calm. She couldn't see Donovan. Of course, her position didn't allow her to see all of the large space and she knew she had to move. She stepped away from her position by the door and tentatively ventured farther into the bar area. She didn't get far when a gentleman stopped in front of her, eyeing her with interest. He spoke to her in rapid Spanish and she didn't need a translator to recognize the hunger in his gaze. She smiled weakly and shook her head no. Whatever he'd asked, she didn't think it would be something that she'd readily agree to, and no doubt, something that Donovan would be murderous over.

She endeavored to look unremarkable as she walked around, keeping her head down and not looking anyone in the eyes. The air conditioning was low, sending cool air rushing over her skin and turning her nipples into hard points. The way they jutted beneath her dress was obscene, and while it was totally acceptable in that environment, it didn't exactly make her inconspicuous. She wondered if Donovan was in a meeting in a back room. She was contemplating whether to go back to the hotel when she saw him.

Her breath stopped in her throat and her stomach clenched. He wore fitted black leather pants, his bare muscular chest was heaving with exertion. His hard jaw and his eyes were cold and unforgiving. He looked totally hot and dominant, *and* relentless. But that's not what had Makayla's chest tightening and her breath halting. It was what he was doing and who he was doing it with.

At his feet, a handcuffed woman knelt while he circled her, a crop held at his side. When he turned, the scarified eagle's wings dominating his back stood out in stark relief under the ultraviolet lights, undulating as his muscles rippled with his movements, making them seem almost real.

Makayla stopped and stared. The image he created was dramatic and literally took her breath away. She realized immediately the true symbolic nature of the eagle's wings to Donovan—they represented everything he was as a Dominant.

Makayla let her gaze drift over the kneeling woman. The woman wore a latex bra and matching miniskirt, a relatively sedate outfit, considering the venue. Red welts criss-crossed her back. She trembled, but Makayla could tell that it wasn't from fear. The submissive was obviously excited, aroused even. Her flushed face, slightly parted lips and her erect nipples easily visible through the latex all indicated her stimulated state. She arched her back, exaggerating her chest. She wore a blindfold and her dark hair formed a soft veil around her bent head. Even to Makayla's untrained eye, she looked beautiful in her submission.

Jealousy, fierce and hot, flared through her, fisting her heart and squeezing, leaving her physically shaking from the intensity. She wanted to take that crop and smack the woman over the head with it. She felt positively violent. Donovan's betrayal and his duplicity were absolute. Only the previous evening she'd been fantasizing about this very thing, imagining Donovan doing these things to *her*. And here he was, wielding that supremacy, that dominance, over another woman.

Makayla watched with blurred vision as he raised the crop and sent it expertly cracking across the woman's back, forcing her to arch farther and moan, but drawing no blood and leaving only the smallest mark. They were surrounded by a group of observers, all watching the scene with acute interest.

The second strike was too much for Makayla to bear and she sobbed loudly, hurt and outrage taking tight hold of her.

Donovan snapped his eyes to hers, wide with confusion then, in a nanosecond, they narrowed with his anger.

Makayla didn't wait around. She needed out of there—and fast. She swung about and headed blindly for the exit, stumbling in her haste. Donovan's loud and emphatic cursing followed her but she didn't pause. Then, incredibly, Fernando appeared at her side—where the fuck had he come from? She didn't know, nor did she care, only that he was the closest person she could call a friend, however loosely.

He grasped her elbow. "Makayla, you're in no state to be alone. I'll take you back to the hotel."

She nodded and leaned on him, allowing him to lead her outside and into a taxi, thankful for his proximity. Her mind raced as she tried to piece together what she'd witnessed and the implications. She was now supremely relieved that she had access to her savings. At least she'd be able to purchase a return ticket. She'd leave everything at the hotel save her few personal items. She didn't want any of the clothes or other things that Donovan had given her and had always intended on returning them to him. She'd only acquiesced where that was concerned because he'd cajoled her into it, playing to her compliant nature.

She really didn't know what to think, her mind a jumble of questions. She *did* know, however, that she felt totally wounded by Donovan's betrayal. Why had he been keeping this from her, hiding his activities and covertly sneaking around? She hoped to God that he hadn't taken his scenes further and into sexual territory — the thought made her physically ill.

Beside her, Fernando placed a reassuring hand on her knee and gave a little squeeze. She smiled weakly at him. At least her tears had subsided, but she must look a frightful mess.

She sighed and leaned her head back, closing her eyes, the events of the evening having exhausted her.

Chapter Twenty-One

Donovan raged. He wanted—no—he *needed* desperately to go after Makayla, but his responsibilities as a Dom left him with few options. Aftercare of a sub was an extremely important aspect to a scene, and he would be remiss in his duty if he just charged out and left the sub to tend to herself. Some Dominants required aftercare too, but Donovan had never gone in for it. He suspected because he felt it challenged his own self-control. Now, he had to waste precious time tending to someone else—

"Fuck!"

The look on Makayla's face had just about broken him. Initially, he'd been confused. Then anger had overtaken him, so visceral that it had left him shaking. How the fuck had she found him and *who* the fuck had let her in?

And where the hell was Fernando? The last time he'd seen him was before Makayla's arrival. Was that motherfucker using Donovan's predicament and Makayla's distress to his advantage? Jealousy gripped him like a vise. If Fernando so much as touched a fucking hair on her head, Donovan would kill him.

He spent half an hour ensuring that the sub was okay, that she felt comfortable and safe. Then he got the hell out of there, hailing a cab to take him directly to the hotel. He'd spent most of that half an hour of aftercare rejecting the sub's advances. She always wanted something more. She'd wanted sexual release from him, even though they had discussed beforehand that it wasn't an option. A while ago, he wouldn't have hesitated. In fact, he would have taken great pleasure from it, but not since Makayla. From the time when she had entered his life, there hadn't been anyone else, only her. Fuck knew what she was thinking now. No doubt that he'd been cheating on her, and in a way, he guessed he had, but not sexually. He'd understood the risks associated with sneaking around behind Makayla's back, but he'd needed the release, the outlet that a BDSM session gave him. He should have fucking listened to his gut instinct. He had to hope that she was still at the hotel, that she didn't have the funds to get herself back to Australia, but knowing Makayla, she'd have factored in the possibility of having to return without him. The five-minute cab ride seemed interminable. Finally, they pulled up outside the Totally Five Star. Donovan threw a ten-euro note at the driver, not waiting for change, and dove out to sprint inside to the elevator bank.

He tore through their suite like a madman—she wasn't there. All of her things looked to be in place so he had to hope that she hadn't left the hotel. Then again, he wouldn't have put it past her to have left all the things he'd given her behind. He'd virtually had to bully her into accepting everything in the first place.

He headed back downstairs and thought about Fernando. He was suspicious as to why that fucker had left Infierno when he had—right after Makayla had fled. Donovan knew he wanted Makayla. He'd been pretty fucking blatant about it, actually.

Donovan barged into Fernando's office and took in the scene. They were sitting side by side on the lounge. Fernando had one arm around Makayla's shoulders and a hand on her knee. Her head was bent close to his as they talked quietly—what the fuck? Rage, hot and heavy, roared through him and punched him in the gut. How dare the prick touch her! In two quick strides, Donovan was looming over them.

"Do you fucking mind?" he grated between clenched teeth, his hands fisted at his sides. "Keep your hands to yourself, motherfucker."

The other man smiled grimly. "It's not a good time, King. Makayla needs a moment."

"She can take a moment in *our* suite," Donovan snarled. "She's coming with me."

Without another word, he bent and snatched her away from the man, scooping her up and into his arms. She didn't struggle, perhaps assuming that it would do no good. It wouldn't. He needed her to hear him out and he would do anything in his power to ensure that happened.

He stalked out of Fernando's office and glanced down at Makayla. Her mouth was set in a mulish line and she refused to meet his eyes. He used his elbow to punch the elevator button, keeping her cradled in his arms.

"I *am* capable of walking, Donovan," she snarled at him.

"I'm well aware of that. But I prefer you in my arms."

"Don't get used to it," she muttered under her breath.

Donovan narrowed his eyes on her but remained silent. Her sullen expression and rigid posture told him not to push things.

He didn't want to stand her on her feet. A strange fear had gripped him, telling him that if he let her go, she'd be gone for good. They arrived at their suite and, holding Makayla with one arm, Donovan swiped the key card, opening the door. He always marveled at how easy it was to carry her. She was so little that he handled her with ease. Good job too, he mused — it meant that he had better control of these unfamiliar situations.

"You can put me down now," she said petulantly.

"Promise me that you won't run," he demanded, holding her tightly against his body.

She huffed out an exasperated sigh. "I won't run."

He looked down at her, assessing her expression then decided that if she did break her promise and run, he could catch her easily. He loosened his hold and allowed her to slide down his body slowly, relishing the feel of her soft curves against his hardness.

She stepped away from him and immediately he mourned her proximity. He had to get a hold of himself. This girl was driving him crazy, making him feel and do things that were previously foreign to him. He shoved a hand through his hair in frustration. "We have to talk," he eventually said. "I need to explain some things."

She eyed him coldly, her expression sending another jab of fear through him

"It's late and I'm tired," she murmured, walking into the bedroom.

"Tomorrow then," he persisted. "You're killing me here, baby. Please give me an indication of what you're thinking."

She turned to face him. "I'm not sure what I'm going to do. I do know that it's too late right now to leave and I have to sleep on some things. I need to be alone at the moment."

"Fuck," he cursed quietly, shoving both hands through his hair and yanking.

"Can you let me sleep in here alone?" she asked, indicating the bedroom.

"Of course." He nodded stiffly and stepped backward over the threshold.

The soft click of the latch could have been a door slamming in his face, for all the finality it implied. He stared around the luxurious combined dining-sitting room, his gaze landing on all the finery but taking nothing in. Finally, he dragged one of the dining room chairs over and positioned it in front of the bedroom door. He couldn't afford to fall asleep and have her leave without him noticing. His relief at finding her still at the hotel was fast diminishing under her impenetrable demeanor.

He looked at his watch—two a.m. He'd sit and wait until morning, keeping guard at the bedroom door, then he'd make her listen to him.

Chapter Twenty-Two

When Makayla woke, the events of the previous evening bombarded her brain and sent questions ricocheting around her head.

She'd slept fitfully, finally deciding in the early hours that she'd listen to what Donovan had to say. She owed him that much, she supposed, and truth be told, *she* needed to know.

She showered and changed into a soft floral summer dress with shoestring straps and a fitted bodice that lifted her bust and hugged her torso, the skirt flaring softly at her hips. It looked feminine and pretty—she hadn't worn it before and it gave her the confidence that she needed to face the morning ahead.

She piled her hair atop her head in a messy bun and applied some light makeup, dusting her lids with a soft shade of mauve to highlight her violet eyes. She knew Donovan loved her eyes and she was determined to make herself look desirable to him. The events of the previous evening had left her feeling insecure and apprehensive and she needed everything in her feminine arsenal to combat the emotions.

She took a deep breath and went to open the bedroom door — it wouldn't budge. *What the fuck?* She rarely swore but this situation warranted it. Had Donovan locked her in?

She rattled the doorknob. It turned, but something was stopping the door from opening. Suddenly, it swung outward to reveal Donovan standing on the other side wearing cargo shorts and a fitted navy T-shirt that molded to his sculpted chest. His hair was wet from a recent shower and the smell of soap and spicy aftershave wafted around him.

"Did you lock me in?" she demanded incredulously.

"Not exactly," he responded, his expression unreadable.

She cocked an eyebrow in inquiry.

"I jammed the door with a chair and that armoire," he explained, indicating a small chest of drawers. "I needed to go to the gym to work off some steam and I didn't want you leaving."

She gaped at him. "What if there had been a fire?"

"I thought of that, angel. There's no way I would ever put you in danger. I had one of the hotel staff posted at the door until I returned."

Makayla wondered what they must have thought about that arrangement, but no doubt, Donovan had paid the person well to keep their silence and their thoughts to themselves.

She watched him warily as he took a step toward her. The raw hunger in his eyes as his gazed traveled the length of her body took her breath away. Talking to him was going to be harder than she'd anticipated when he looked at her like that.

"You're beautiful," he said huskily, extending an arm toward her, his hand outstretched for her to take. But she just gazed at him, not yet willing to allow him to touch her. She was afraid that if she made contact with him her resolve would crumble.

"Please, Makayla," he pleaded. "I need to touch you."

"Let's just talk for the moment. I have some questions."

He sighed and dropped his arm to his side. "Of course. I had José deliver breakfast." He indicated the dining room table, spread with a delicious array of pastries.

She took a seat. Donovan sat opposite, studying her warily and pouring them each juice and coffee.

Makayla inhaled deeply. "Why did you hide" — she paused, trying to find the right word — "your pastime from me?"

He leaned back in his chair and gave her a serious look. "I didn't want to expose you to that world — to my world. You're so pure and innocent. You don't belong there. Also, I was worried that you'd run. That you'd think me obscene and immoral." He laughed grimly. "I virtually had to tie you down to stop you from running away from me, so I wasn't too far off the mark there." He sighed. "How did you find me?"

She blushed and stared into her lap. "I followed you. I didn't believe your explanations for all these late-night meetings."

Donovan nodded. "I should have realized that you'd be suspicious. You have to try to understand, Makayla, it's an outlet for me, as well as many other things."

She looked up from her lap, curious to know just what it was about the BDSM lifestyle that drew Donovan. "Why?" she asked simply.

He sighed and ran a hand through his hair. "It's hard to explain, but it's very much about self-control and my ability to control others, to read the submissive's desires and needs, and to react to those needs responsibly and knowledgeably. To question and predict what they need from me next. I have a dominant personality, Makayla. You should have realized that by now. Managing my self-discipline is very important to me." He seemed pained. "Although I have to question my ability since you've come into my life. You're the one person who can send me adrift. I have to work harder to retain control, which is at once heady and exhilarating in its challenge, and beyond fucking frustrating."

She frowned. "I don't understand how I can do that to you. How do *I* affect your self-control?"

He gave her an incredulous stare. "Holding onto my willpower where you're concerned has been a struggle, to say the least. For Christ's sake, Makayla, I can't stand another man even looking at you, let alone talking to you. It makes me feel crazy, violently so, knowing that they want what's mine. I've never felt this way before and I'm worried that my self-control will suffer because of it." He laughed bitterly. "This is unfamiliar territory and it infuriates the fuck out of me. I've needed the release and the validation that I find at Infierno. I've needed to prove to myself that I haven't lost the edge, that I'm still the master of restraint."

Makayla didn't know what to say, dismayed that she could make him feel that way. "I'm sorry," was all she could manage.

"Don't apologize, baby. It's something that *I* need to deal with. It's my problem."

She studied him across the table, formulating her next question. "I know a little about the BDSM lifestyle. Sometimes that control and the D/s dynamic involve a sexual release." She gazed down at the table, hating to ask, but unable to stop herself. "Did you...do that with the submissive?"

When he remained silent, she peeked up at him. He stared at her, a frown crossing his features. "I didn't realize that you knew anything about BDSM. Are you holding back on me, angel?" His eyes glinted dangerously. "And you'd better not tell me that you've experienced anything first-hand because I'll be needing some answers."

"No," she cried, aghast. "I stumbled across something on your computer." She paused. "It intrigued me, that's all."

He breathed a sigh of relief, his body visibly relaxing. "Well, you have been busy," he murmured and gave her a level look. "To answer your question, it doesn't always involve sex and no, I haven't touched anyone else sexually since I met you. You have to believe me. In fact, I'm not interested in anyone else like that—at all."

Makayla believed him. Fernando had intimated as much, telling her not to think the worst about what she'd seen. Also, if Donovan's sexual frustration after returning from his stints at Infierno were anything to go by, he definitely hadn't been dabbling.

"Did you in the past?"

"Yes. In the past a BDSM scene for me always involved consensual sex."

A sick feeling swept through her at the thought of Donovan with so many women, and the things he must have done with those women. She shook her head to rid herself of the images.

"Why do they call you the King of Infierno?"

He shifted in his seat, looking uncomfortable suddenly. "It's a play on my name, I guess, and I've been in the scene for a long time. Others in the scene like to…observe my techniques, learn from me." He shrugged. "At the risk of sounding egotistical, I'm a good Dominant. Submissives want me to train them, to nurture them. I suppose you could say that I'm sought after." He chuckled grimly. "It's not a moniker that I encourage, or even wanted. It just happened."

She took a sip of coffee, tepid after sitting for so long, and traced an invisible pattern on the tabletop, not wanting to meet Donovan's eyes when she asked her next question. "Do you think I'd make a good submissive?"

He was silent for a long moment as she continued to avoid his gaze.

"Yes," he eventually said, his voice low and husky. "You'd make a perfect submissive."

She felt his gaze burning into her and she lifted her head. His eyes, swimming with lust and desire, bore into hers, even as he shook his head. "But you won't ever be involved in that lifestyle, so stop asking these questions."

A flare of anger shot through her at his words. What was so wrong with her? "Then I've made my decision. I want to leave here now. I want to go home."

"*What*? Why would you say that? I've answered your questions truthfully. Do you want me to promise never to go to a BDSM club again? To wipe all of that out of my life?"

She shook her head. "No. It's part of who you are."

"Well, what then? What do you want me to do, Makayla? Because I'll do it, I won't lose you."

"I *hated* seeing you with that woman," she said, her voice shaking with emotion. "I was so jealous of her."

Donovan shot her an incredulous look. "Why would you be jealous of her? I hate that you saw that part of me. That was not for your eyes."

She huffed in exasperation. "I'm not some naïve little girl, Donovan. What are you trying to protect me from?"

"From me," he said simply. "From that lifestyle. I don't want your innocence influenced by it."

She arched an eyebrow. "You have to stop thinking of me like that. What if I told you that I want to be a part of it?"

He drew his breath in sharply. "That's not a good idea, Makayla."

She lifted her chin in defiance. "It's my decision." She knew her next words would hit him where he was most vulnerable. "If you won't help me, perhaps someone else will."

He growled low in his throat, the sound so threatening that it sent a shiver of fear rippling through her.

"Don't even fucking joke about that," he said dangerously. "You know that I can't abide the thought of anyone else touching you, let alone dominating you. It's not fucking happening, Makayla."

"Then you'll give me what I want." She knew that she was poking the proverbial bear, but it was the only way she could think of to make him see things her way.

He shook his head. "And you're supposed to be submissive?" he asked. "Submissives don't generally make the demands, angel. They do what they're told. They hold the power but they don't make the decisions."

"Will you train me?" she asked quietly. "To be a submissive?"

He stood suddenly and was in front of her in two strides, pulling her up from her chair and into his arms. He cupped the cheeks of her ass and tugged her into him, bending his knees to reach where he needed to grind his hard cock into her pelvis, sending little shock waves to her core. He dipped his head and brushed his lips across hers, speaking directly against her mouth.

"You don't know how many times I've imagined dominating you, how I've thought about you submitting to me entirely, having you totally under my control." As he spoke, his cock grew harder, responding to his words and throbbing between them, hot and insistent. "I've craved that from you, but at the same time, I've kicked myself for thinking it of you at all." He swept his mouth across hers, slowly and sensually. "I don't want to spoil you. You're my beautiful angel, my pure sweet girl. Tell me why you want it," he demanded softly.

She moaned into his mouth and threw her arms around his neck. He picked her up, her legs dangling off the floor, and gripped her behind to nestle his cock more precisely and firmly against her soft core. His words and the insistent throbbing of his erection made it impossible for her to think straight through her lust for him.

"Answer me, baby," he murmured against her lips, rubbing delicious little circles with his pelvis.

"I want to give up control. I don't want to make the decisions anymore," she mumbled dreamily. "I saw those submissives online, giving control to a Dominant. Letting the Dominant take the lead and make the choices." She paused, allowing him to massage her lips more forcefully with his own. "It made me...hot," she finished breathlessly.

He groaned and took her in a deep, passionate kiss and forced her legs around his waist, pulling her down to press against his cock, hitting her center perfectly.

"Please, Donovan," she begged.

"First lesson, angel," he said. "You don't call the shots anymore." He ground more forcefully against her. "You sure you want to do this?"

"Yes," she panted, squirming and trying desperately to hit *that* spot.

"Stop wriggling. I'm going to take you now. We won't be doing anything else until we discuss your training further."

He walked them to the bedroom, where he lowered them both to the bed. He dragged her dress up to her waist, exposing her pink lace G-string.

"Now I'm going to taste you," he breathed into her flesh as he kissed his way down her belly.

Makayla held her breath, waiting anxiously, then suddenly he was there, running his index finger along her slit through the satin of her panties. She bucked beneath him.

"I can tell that you're wet for me," he muttered, his breath hot against the sensitive flesh of her inner thigh. "Your panties are damp with your arousal."

She moaned and opened her legs wider, inviting more from him.

He slipped his finger under the elastic of her G-string and rubbed circles along her folds, spreading her moisture around and locating her clit. Tremors of pleasure shot through her as he fondled the little bundle of nerves. He plunged two fingers inside her and pushed high and deep, forcing her to bow off the bed.

"Donovan," she cried out, quivers wracking her body as he massaged her G-spot.

He withdrew his fingers slowly, smirking as he lifted them to his lips and sucked. "Hmm, you taste divine. My favorite flavor. Take off your dress and panties," he ordered, his voice a low rumble.

She hurried to do his bidding and quickly stripped down to nothing. Donovan did the same, toeing off his Vans and shrugging out of his shorts, boxer briefs and T-shirt until he was standing gloriously naked in front of her.

"We're going to try something different," he explained, climbing onto the bed and lying on his back. "I want you to straddle me. Sit on my face, this way." He grasped her hips and positioned her on top of him. "Now sit."

It was a vulnerable position, but she swallowed her nerves and did as he asked, lowering herself gingerly to his face. She moaned when she felt his mouth collide with her pussy and his tongue delve deeply into her channel.

"Oh, fuck," she grunted. The sensation was overwhelming and so different. She sat facing his hard cock, the crown swollen and purple, beads of milky liquid oozing from his tip. She leaned forward and grasped his shaft, making him buck beneath her. She licked the tip, lapping hungrily at his pre-cum and squeezing more out of him.

He groaned into her folds, sending delicious vibrations directly to her core. She trembled, her inner muscles contracting and pulsing as he fucked her with his mouth.

She closed her lips around him and sucked hard, using her fist to pump the root of his cock and relaxing her jaw to take more of him deeper into her throat.

He sucked on her clit and thrust two fingers into her quivering hole. She cried out and ground herself into his face, feeling the pleasure starting to build and tighten within her.

She allowed his cock to slip between her lips and fisted it quickly, using her saliva to lubricate her glide.

"Yes," she cried. "I'm close!"

He jerked his hips up, a silent request to take him in her mouth once more. She sucked his shaft and slid him deeper, feeling him brush the back of her throat. She stiffened and held her breath, squeezing the root of him and fisting him rapidly.

Then she was there, at the edge of that wonderful abyss, her core quivering and pulsing as she tumbled over the edge and waves of euphoria swept through her, sending her vision hazy and the blood roaring through her ears.

Beneath her, Donovan growled into her pussy and gripped her hips as he pushed himself deeper into her throat and emptied inside her in long, thick bursts.

Chapter Twenty-Three

Donovan awoke with a throbbing cock. It was hard and insistent. Just thinking and dreaming about Makayla submitting to him was driving him wild with lust. Of course, she'd always been compliant, perfectly so, but there was a difference between compliance and pure submission. Against his better judgment, he was going to train her. Fuck, what choice did she give him? Either he agreed, or she'd find another Dominant, and he knew that there'd be a long list of fucking assholes ready and willing. The mere thought of it made his blood boil. There was no way he would allow anyone else to touch her, particularly not in *that* way. He only trusted himself in that capacity.

He knew he was a good Dominant, one of the best at reading his submissives and predicting how far to take them, what they needed and when. He couldn't deny that the thought of having Makayla in *every* way was a huge turn-on. He was going to be her first for so many experiences — it truly was a gift. He'd been reluctant to admit it before, but he would now — she was precious to him. He wouldn't give her up for anything.

Before the events of the previous night and their chat that morning, he'd been loath to address his feelings, worried that if she discovered the real Donovan, she'd run from him, and he'd convinced himself that it would be better for her in the end. Things were different now and the goalposts had moved. Now he was aware of her true desires—albeit desires that Makayla had only recently discovered in herself—but needs, just the same. He would be the man to fulfill those needs for her—him and only him—and her training would begin today.

* * * *

Makayla awoke from her nap to find her wrists tied to the bedframe, Donovan standing beside her and staring down, his expression impassive. A flutter of fear and anxiety hit her belly and spread outward. This was Donovan in Dominant mode, and the sight both intimidated and thrilled her. He wore only his cargo shorts, his glorious chest bare and heaving with his deep breathing.

"Do you understand safe words, baby?" he asked, his voice rough.

"Yes. I read about them."

"Good. That's very important. You have to appreciate that you hold the ultimate power here. I can't do anything that you don't want me to do. I can't take you further than you can handle. As your Dom, it's my responsibility to understand you, to read your wants and desires, to predict your needs. That's where safe words come in. If you can't handle something or don't like something, and God forbid that I've misread you, you say your safe word and I stop immediately. Do you understand?"

She nodded.

"Answer me, angel,"

"Yes, I understand."

"Yes, what?"

She looked at him in confusion. What else did he want from her?

He smirked. "You call me Sir, Master or Mr. King. Take your pick."

She gave him a wide-eyed look. Was he serious?

He chuckled. "Look at those beautiful violet eyes shimmering with confusion and uncertainty. It makes me hard just looking at you like that. This is part of the deal, baby. You can't choose some bits and leave out others. A D/s relationship is all or nothing, at least it is for me."

"I'm sorry, Sir," she whispered.

He grinned triumphantly, his eyes glittering with raw hunger. "That's my girl. Now, what is your safe word? You can choose anything."

She couldn't think. Her mind was in a jumble, excitement and anticipation warming her blood. She'd read something about safe words and decided that the most common one was the easiest. "Red," she said. "I know it's boring, but I can't think of anything else."

"Well, I'm hoping that you won't ever have to use it, so boring doesn't matter as long as you remember it. I'm going to go easy on you, baby. This is your first experience with BDSM. I need to recognize your limits, your desires and your needs — that won't happen overnight." He bent and slipped a finger between her wrist and the scarf that he'd used to bind her. "Is it too tight?"

"No, Sir."

"Good. Today we use scarves. Later, we'll graduate to handcuffs and other things." He produced a black scarf from his pocket. "I'm going to blindfold you now. I want you to focus on what I'm doing to you."

He tied the material around her head, covering her eyes. Her heart rate sped up as anxiety trickled down her spine.

"Relax, baby," he coaxed soothingly.

Music started playing, something soft and sensual that she didn't recognize. She deepened her breathing and calmed her hammering heart, allowing the music to wash over her.

She gasped as a sharp pain centered on her nipple— Donovan pinching her.

"Is that too much?" he murmured, his breath hot at her ear.

"No, Sir."

The pain increased, sending sharp tingles shooting directly to her core. She groaned and arched her back.

"Nipple clamps will work well for you," he stated with satisfaction. His fingers were replaced with something warm and wet—his mouth as he sucked her tortured nipple, laving the turgid peak with his tongue.

"Oh, fuck," she muttered, and was rewarded with a swift slap to her thigh.

"Oh, baby. Curse words coming out of that sweet little mouth is paradoxical. Like an angel being bad. I hate it and love it at the same time." His breath warmed the damp flesh where his tongue had been, peaking her nipple further. "Don't go overboard with the dirty mouth, though. I don't want to punish you already."

She felt the mattress shift as he climbed onto the bed.

"Stay still. If you move, I'll bind your legs. Don't come until I tell you to."

Suddenly his mouth was on her pussy, sucking and licking, his tongue twirling around her clit relentlessly. She arched beneath him, forgetting his instructions.

"Don't move," he demanded against her core. "You need to absorb the pleasure and control your reactions."

She struggled to stay still, the vibrations of his voice against her center and his swirling tongue too much. She breathed deeply, trying to work through the sensations gripping her insides.

He added a finger, plunging in and out of her so she could hear her slickness, even over the music. He added another finger and used his tongue to massage her clit, sucking it into his mouth.

Oh God, she was close. Her internal muscles tightened, signaling her imminent orgasm. She couldn't hold on any longer and just when she was about to give in, to allow the sweet release to take hold, Donovan pulled away. She moaned in frustration as her impending orgasm receded, leaving in its wake an unfulfilled throbbing.

"I know when you're close, baby." His voice was at her ear again. "You tense your muscles, your breath hitches and I can feel the pulses start in your sweet pussy. You also hold your breath—did you realize that? You were going to disobey me. You were very close to giving in to your desires and you were going to come without my permission, weren't you?"

She didn't answer. She was too busy trying to control the raging need swamping her. She wanted to cross her legs, but she knew he wouldn't like that. The throbbing in her core was an ache now and not a pleasant one, almost painful as it radiated throughout her lower belly.

"Answer me," he demanded.

"Yes, Sir," she sobbed. "I was going to come."

Suddenly he flipped her over onto her stomach, the binding at her wrists allowing it easily. She gasped in surprise as he lifted her hips, raising her ass in the air.

"Keep your elbows on the bed," he ordered from behind her.

She felt him massage her cheeks, his palm large, flat and seeming impossibly big against her backside.

"Remember your safe word," he instructed. "I'm going to spank you. It's also a test to see how much you can take, comfortably. If it's too much, you need to say your safe word. You were going to disobey me, so you need to control your responsiveness." He chuckled, still running a hand over the cheeks of her ass. "Don't get me wrong, I fucking love that you're so responsive to me, but you need to learn to manage it, angel. Or it will control you, and trust me, when it comes, when that release finally barrels down on you, it will be that much sweeter."

A frisson of fear mixed with excitement rippled down her spine. He was going to spank her. She was nervous but pleasantly so—she wanted this. She wanted something similar to what Donovan had so easily given to that submissive at the club.

Suddenly, he slapped her ass, hard. She yelped and jumped, the shock more than any pain causing her to gasp. He followed the first with three quick successive smacks, the sharp tingles radiating outward. He slid his hand across her ass, soothing and massaging the sting.

"How many?" he murmured. "I think ten will suffice. Are you okay?"

She nodded.

He slapped her again on the right cheek then on the left, alternating the smacks and never quite hitting the same spot twice. She wriggled as a pleasurable heat spread through her. She enjoyed being spanked, enjoyed the bite of pain and the feel of his palm on her backside.

"Your ass is so pink now, baby. So beautifully warmed by me." His voice was tight with need.

His last slap landed on the juncture between her thighs, forcing a low moan from deep in her throat. He sank two fingers into her and groaned. "You're so wet. You liked the spanking. Not much of a punishment if you liked it."

He continued to plunge his fingers in and out of her, her slickness causing squelching noises. "Oh fuck," he muttered. "I have to have you. I give you permission to come."

She felt him on the mattress behind her, then he was slamming into her, plunging balls deep until she was sure he'd hit her cervix. They groaned in unison. He was so deep it was almost painful. He withdrew to the tip and plunged again, hard. That was it, she was so worked up the orgasm hit her without lead-up or warning. Suddenly her insides convulsed, undulating and contracting around his thick cock. She shuddered and cried out as the ecstasy washed over her, sending waves of pleasure rippling outward. He picked up the tempo, grasping her hips and yanking her back onto his erection, growling like a wild animal. She allowed him to manipulate her body, twisting and jerking her until, with a load groan in her ear, he was shooting deep inside her, calling her name, shuddering and rotating his hips as he worked through his orgasm.

Chapter Twenty-Four

Donovan stared down at a sleeping Makayla. She was exhausted and he was very close to fucking her to death. He couldn't seem to keep his hands to himself around her.

While she'd been napping that afternoon, he'd slipped out and had gone to Chueca to one of his favorite sex shops. He'd discuss it further with her over dinner, but he needed to be sure that she wanted to experiment in BDSM for the right reasons and not just because she thought it was what he wanted. If she was serious about the submissive training, then he wanted to initiate her into using toys, slowly and with no big leaps. The idea sent an erotic thrill coursing through him, forcing his cock to stand at attention and tightening his balls. The idea of his sweet, innocent angel wearing nipple clamps and a butt plug was enough to make him come on the spot. He scrubbed a hand through his hair. Shit, he had to get a hold of himself. He was acting like a fucking virgin schoolboy.

He strode to the walk-in closet and chose a dress for Makayla, a deep purple, a color he loved her in. The plunging, almost non-existent neckline that the personal shopper seemed to have an obsession with would complement her pert breasts perfectly. The style was different, almost Grecian. The wide fabric straps connected directly to the waistline and formed the covering for the breasts, going up directly over the shoulders and connecting with the waist at the back. It was calf-length and made of some sort of floaty fabric. He couldn't wait to see her in it.

He wandered back into the bedroom and knelt by the bed, brushing Makayla's hair off her forehead.

"Wake up, baby," he said softly and dropped a kiss on her lips.

She moaned and fluttered her lids, finally focusing her sleepy, gorgeous eyes on him. "What time is it?" she asked.

Her usual husky voice, made huskier from sleep, sent a lightning bolt straight to his cock.

She sat up and yawned, stretching her arms above her head and dislodging the sheet. It pooled around her waist, exposing her creamy breasts, peaked by tight red nipples. He groaned, his mouth watering. He loved her breasts and they fit perfectly in his hands. He adored the plump feel of them in his mouth as he sucked them.

"It's eight o'clock. You have to have a shower, angel." Longing tightened his voice. "If you don't get out of that bed now, I'll be joining you in it and we'll miss dinner."

She dove out of bed, her tight little ass swaying sexily as she made her way to the bathroom. He'd turned the water on already and had contemplated joining her, but decided against it, knowing that it would make them late, and he supposed that he should give her a break from his cock for a while.

They'd been in bed for most of the day and they needed some fresh air and a change of scenery.

He leaned against the bathroom wall and watched her soaping herself—crazy, really, given that he wanted nothing more than to dive on her again—but it was a personal test in self-control. He'd watch her and crave her, but he wouldn't do anything about it, for now at least.

She turned to face him, running soapy circles around her belly with the sponge. White, frothy bubbles slid down her tummy and hips to catch in the blonde curls between her thighs. Fuck, this was a huge lesson in restraint. His shaft throbbed and ached to be buried inside her sweet, tight cunt. He lifted his gaze to her breasts and watched, almost mesmerized, as creamy soapsuds dripped from her erect nipples like drops of cum. Next time he fucked her, he decided, he'd come all over her plump breasts.

"You know, no one has ever watched me shower before," she murmured in her husky voice.

He leveled a hard stare at her. "I should fucking hope not."

He straightened and stepped toward the open cubicle then raised his hands to grasp the bar across the top, his bare chest bulging and rippling.

She gave him a lust-filled look and licked her full, pouty lips.

"Just remember, baby," he said, his voice low and menacing. "I'll be the *only* one to ever see this gorgeous sight."

She huffed a breath out at him and rolled her eyes. He'd have to nip that little habit in the bud if she wanted to be his submissive. Good little submissives didn't eye-roll their Doms. He knew she was exasperated at his possessiveness, and truth be told, he didn't know why he felt like he needed to remind her that *he* was the only one for her, but he did. He'd never felt so insecure before, as if at any moment someone was going to take her away from him, or she'd leave of her own accord, and that possibility scared the shit out of him. To give himself some semblance of security, he reminded her at every possible opportunity that she was *his*. He would also have to acknowledge that he belonged to her, irrecoverably so. He couldn't imagine another woman would come close to making him feel like Makayla did. Once he'd tasted, and taken, that sweet innocence, he was done for—she'd ruined him for other women. She was smart, gorgeous, sweet, compliant... The list went on, his perfect woman wrapped up in a phenomenal sexy package. No wonder he was so fucking insecure where she was concerned. She had that thing, that unnamable something that men and women alike couldn't seem to ignore. Men lusted after her and women stared with a mixture of jealousy and fascination.

Donovan shook himself out of his reverie and walked into the bedroom to finish getting ready.

Makayla emerged from the bathroom some minutes later. She'd twisted her hair into a large topknot and applied light makeup, highlighting her eyes. He studied her and decided that he approved of her hair. He'd initially envisioned it left down and cascading around her shoulders, but he liked the quirkiness of the topknot.

He pointed to the bed where he'd laid out her dress and selected a pair of very high, strappy heels with Jimmy Choo written on the insole. Donovan had no idea who the hell Jimmy was but he definitely liked his fuck-me heels.

Makayla quirked an eyebrow at him. "You've chosen what you want me to wear?"

"Yes. Don't question it, angel."

She shrugged. "I don't mind. It makes it easier for me and the dress is lovely." She stopped and gave him a flirty look, batting her eyelashes. "I also like that I'll be wearing something you chose for me."

In two strides, he was standing in front of her. He whipped the towel from her body and grasped her around her upper arms, pulling her into him. He bent his head to hers and kissed her, snaking his tongue out to lick the seam of her lips, tasting strawberries. "Oh, fuck," he groaned. "You taste so good."

She giggled sweetly. "It's my lip gloss."

"Well, tell me what brand it is and I'll buy a truckload. I can't get enough of you." He deepened the kiss, bending her backward over his arm and delving into her mouth with his tongue. Finally, he straightened and gazed down at her, grinning at her heavy-lidded, lust-filled gaze. He steadied her on her feet and slapped her backside. "Get dressed, and no underwear."

"What?"

"You heard me. It's quite common, baby, and you've done it before. I'm sure half the women in the restaurant won't be wearing underwear and no one could tell. But I'll know my girl isn't wearing any and it'll drive me fucking wild. Having you sitting next to me with nothing between us but the fabric of your dress... It's another test to my willpower. I'm determined to push my limits."

Donovan left her to finish getting dressed and waited for her in the sitting room. He was checking his text messages when she emerged a few minutes later, and his breath hitched at the sight of her. She looked stunning, as usual. The dress fit her perfectly and he could see her navel and the smooth skin of her flat stomach. Her breasts pillowed out of the sides of the gathered straps slightly, giving a glimpse of what lay underneath. Shit, what was he thinking, encouraging her to wear that?

She spun around, her skirt flaring out around her shapely legs, showing off the blonde curls at the juncture of her thighs and the rounded cheeks of her ass.

He stood. "You will *not* be doing that outside of this suite." *Fuck me, if she does that anywhere else but in front of me, I'll end up killing someone.*

"*You* didn't want me to wear panties," she reminded him.

"I'm well aware of that. Just remember that you aren't wearing any, so no impromptu pirouettes." He stepped toward her and cupped the cheeks of her ass, tugging her into him and rubbing his erection into her soft core. Her sky-high heels made her taller, so he didn't need to bend his knees and pick her up as he usually did to get her just where he wanted her — against his hard cock. He ground against her, moaning low in his throat.

"If you keep doing that I'm going to ruin my dress," she breathed. "You're making me wet."

"Christ, baby. I could take you right here, right now."

"Do it," she pleaded into his mouth.

He shook his head. "No. We have your training to discuss and it's best done over dinner." He spun her around so her ass cheeks were pillowing his cock and slipped his hand around to her front and under her dress, delving a finger deep inside her tight, hot pussy. He thrust in and out for a moment then removed his finger and ran her moisture around the lips of her cunt. She fell against him in limp compliance, gyrating her hips in encouragement.

He chuckled. "Time to go, angel. We'll be late. I just have one more thing to do."

Chapter Twenty-Five

Donovan looked delectable in black jeans, a light gray dress shirt and a black blazer. His hair roguishly mussed with a five o'clock shadow on his jaw gave him that really hot edge that she loved. Makayla stared at him as he drew a long box out of the inside pocket of his jacket.

"A present for you." He handed her the box.

Makayla took it from him and untied the ribbon. Inside, nestled in tissue paper, was... She didn't know what it was. There were two bullet-shaped objects connected to a fine silver chain by long leather loops. She picked it up, her brow furrowing with her confusion.

Donovan smiled and took it from her to drape it around her neck. He looped it once then allowed the bullet-shaped droplets to hang on either side. He then untied the straps of her dress, exposing her breasts, and bent forward, sucking a nipple into his mouth and drawing on it deeply. Makayla moaned, feeling the sensation acutely in her core, as if there was a live wire connected directly to her clit. He pulled away and performed the same action on her other breast then stood and examined his handiwork, her nipples now pointing high and erect. He positioned the leather loops of the necklace over each of her turgid little peaks and tightened them. Finally, he fixed the straps of her dress back in place.

"It's a necklace," Makayla announced triumphantly. Although, why most of it was covered by her dress, and attached to her nipples, no less, she didn't understand.

He took a step back and placed his hand in his pocket. "Not just a necklace."

Suddenly the necklace started to vibrate. Makayla gasped as little bolts of pleasure attacked her nipples.

Donovan grinned. "It's a vibrating droplet necklace. I want you to wear it tonight and I have the controls." He held up a small box and the vibrations stopped as quickly as they'd started. "I had them rig it to be controlled remotely. I thought it would be more…enjoyable to catch you by surprise."

Makayla frowned. "Does it look obvious?" she asked dubiously, walking to the full-length mirror to study her reflection before turning back to Donovan.

His gaze heated and zeroed in on her nipples. "No," he assured her in a tight voice. "I, of course, know it's there, and it'll be another thing to drive me crazy, but to everyone else, it will look like a standard necklace." He lifted his gaze to meet her eyes. "Let's go. We're late."

Makayla walked next to Donovan, his hand on the small of her back. She was getting used to his possessive gestures, not that keeping a hand on her was possessive. It was quite sweet, really, but his hard glare toward any man who happened to look in her direction was slightly over the top. She smiled to herself. He really did act like such a caveman sometimes, and she wondered if he was like this with any of the other women he'd gone out with. She had to work hard not to fidget and be too self-conscious about her outrageous piece of jewelry.

The restaurant was decorated in a contemporary style, the colors muted and neutral. Understated and sophisticated were the two adjectives that stuck in Makayla's brain. All the tables offered privacy and a wonderful view of the city. The patrons were all dressed elegantly, and Makayla noticed the women wearing designs from the likes of Prada and Luis Vuitton, the designer side of her personality suddenly on high alert to the fashions. The staff were all dressed professionally in black and white, their bow ties knotted to perfection as they scurried around unobtrusively ensuring that all the guests had what they needed.

The maître d' showed them to a table in the corner, which had a fabulous view over the city and the park, and a rounded bench seat on one side, ensuring that both diners could enjoy the vista. He placed two glasses of *cava* in front of them, a plate of bite-sized crab *croquetas* and a bowl of marinated olives. A string quartet was playing on a stage in the corner of the room, providing soft ambient music.

"I took the liberty of ordering for us earlier," Donavan told her. "I hope you don't mind, but I wanted you to try the *paella* here and it's better if the chef has prior notice."

"Of course," she responded enthusiastically. "I've been wanting to try it." She took a sip of her *cava* and studied Donovan thoughtfully. "Are you always so possessive of the women you go out with?" she finally asked.

He looked surprised. He leaned back, elbow on the armrest, using his thumb and forefinger to rub his chin, his eyes narrowed pensively. "Actually, no. Well, not in the same way."

Makayla cocked an eyebrow. "In what way, then?"

He breathed out audibly. "I've only ever had two semi-serious relationships and those were not relationships in the traditional sense. They were both long-term submissives. As a Dominant, I tend to be a little possessive, but more protective of my submissive. I need to be confident that she is comfortable, that I understand what she needs, and most of all, that I can ensure her safety and wellbeing. I was protective to that extent, and if my submissive, through mutual consent, wanted to play with another Dominant, then I was definitely protective over her and I would only allow that to go ahead when I was confident with the experience and habits of the other Dominant." He sighed. "Makayla, you're the first woman I've explored anything other than a D/s relationship with. And I don't know what it is, but I'm totally different with you. I'm possessive, bordering on crazy where you're concerned. Ever since I first met you, I've wanted you and, as you know, I stopped at nothing to get you over here with me. With you, I'm possessive, protective and dominant in *and* out of the bedroom. I know I fuck up sometimes, but it's because I don't know how to deal with these unfamiliar feelings and this…situation. Also, to be brutally honest, I never thought that I'd be interested in vanilla sex, but since you, that's changed as well." He grimaced. "You see how *everything* about us is new to me too?"

Makayla shook her head in astonishment. It was the most that Donovan had ever revealed about his feelings for her, and she suspected that he'd surprised himself too. She had so many questions. She took a sip of *cava*, trying to gather her thoughts, and was thankful when their waiter arrived with their shared starter of *ensalada de pulpo*. She smiled at Donovan's fondness for ordering shared plates.

"I hope you like octopus," he murmured, piling her plate with salad then handing it to her. "It really is very good here."

"I like to try everything that you recommend."

Donovan smiled his appreciation, and they were quiet for a few minutes, each enjoying the starter. The octopus was very good, moist and barbecued to perfection, and accompanied by a fresh salad of lettuce, red onion and olives.

Makayla put down her knife and fork. Something that Donovan had said intrigued her. "You said with me you're dominant in *and* out of the bedroom. What did you mean by that?"

Donovan pushed his plate aside and took a sip of *cava*. "With my submissives, I was only ever dominant in a scene or when we fucked. Outside of those two environments, I really didn't mind what they did. Of course, monogamy was expected on both sides unless otherwise arranged and agreed. But as to their day-to-day lives, what they wore, who they associated with..." He shrugged. "It didn't bother me. With you, I'm different. I want to control everything that you do. I'm trying to get a handle on it—hence my visits to Infierno. I need to validate my self-control. I need to assure myself that I am still the master of self-discipline." He sat back in his chair, giving her a level look. "The difference is that I care for you, more than I've cared for anyone before."

Makayla's heart stuttered at his proclamation. She'd been hoping and wishing that he felt something similar for her to what she felt for him. Of course, she hadn't said it yet. She was still too new to this relationship thing, but Donovan was too. It was time that she shared her feelings with him.

"I care for you too," she said softly, placing her hand on his on the table. "And, it might sound silly, but I don't mind your possessiveness and protectiveness. I guess I've spent so long caring for my mother that it's nice to have someone watching out for me." She dropped her gaze. "I'm not sure if that means that I'm weak, or silly, or naïve"—she looked up—"but it's how I feel. I like the sense that someone is attentive to my interests. I feel like… I can finally relax."

Donovan squeezed her hand. "I'm happy to hear you say that, baby, because I can't seem to help myself where you're concerned. But I need you to tell me when you think I'm being unreasonable." He gave her a pointed look. "You know, that's what a lot of people appreciate about being a submissive. That someone they trust is making the decisions for them. That someone else is taking control."

The waiter arrived, and with a flourish, placed a steaming pan of *paella valenciana* between them. The aroma had Makayla's mouth watering in anticipation.

"This *paella* is the traditional style, from Valencia. Made with chicken, rabbit, snails and green beans," Donovan explained as he spooned *paella* onto her plate.

Makayla took a forkful of the flavored rice and moaned in appreciation. The meat tasted moist and delicious. She hadn't been convinced about the snails, but they were quite pleasant to eat. "This is very good. The taste reminds me of Spain," she said in appreciation.

Donovan turned serious. "Makayla, I need you to be very sure that trying the D/s lifestyle is really what you want. You should be aware of what it entails, you have to trust me, and communication between the Dominant and the submissive is extremely important. You have to ensure that you tell me what is too much for you, what you don't like and what you might be willing to try. Often, it involves a contract detailing rules and stipulations and responsibilities of both parties so there are no gray areas, ensuring that the Dominant and the submissive are well aware of each other's desires and limitations."

Makayla put down her fork. "A contract?" she asked incredulously. "Is that really necessary?"

"It's not essential. Some people prefer to have one in place. As long as you communicate with me and tell me what you're thinking and feeling, and you're truthful with me, particularly if we're involved in a scene, then we could progress without one. We'll start slowly, of course. I'm not going to overwhelm you, and I won't take you further than I think you can handle. But you must promise to be communicative and honest with me. If you can't do that, it won't work. I will, of course, do the same for you."

Makayla took a sip of *cava* and studied Donovan thoughtfully. "I trust you," she said. "I'd trust you with my life. I know we haven't known each other for that long, but it's something instinctual. And I want this. When I stumbled across that website then explored further, something came over me." Heat rose in her cheeks at the admission. She was still unused to talking about such intimate things, but she supposed she'd have to overcome that reticence very quickly if Donovan needed her to be vocal about these subjects. "I was intrigued and excited about what I saw…" She looked down at the tabletop. "And aroused, and when I saw you dominating that submissive at the club, I was angry and hurt and jealous but also… I wanted to *be* her."

She lifted her head and met his gaze, his eyes glimmering hungrily in the candlelight. They stared at each other for a long moment, neither of them acknowledging the waiter clearing their table.

"You're catching on quickly, baby," he finally said. "You're being honest about your feelings and talking to me."

Makayla smiled then jerked when little vibrations suddenly attacked her nipples. She'd completely forgotten about the necklace, having grown accustomed to the feeling of it beneath her dress. She gulped, her gaze shooting to Donovan's smirking face.

"Deal with it, angel. Accept the sensations and realize the pleasure," Donovan ordered.

She breathed deeply and willed herself to still. The tingling grew in intensity, zapping the hard little peaks of her breasts with bursts of sensation. It was as if her nipples were hardwired directly to her clit, and she experienced the feeling low in her belly. She couldn't help the soft moan that escaped her throat as desire built in her core and moisture pooled between her thighs. She shifted in her seat, squeezing her legs together to try to seek some relief.

"Your nipples are very sensitive," Donavan murmured. "I like that, that's good. Stop squirming."

She stilled again in her seat and took a couple of deep breaths. The sensations swamping her were becoming unbearable. She should have felt embarrassed, having her nipples so thoroughly attacked in public, but she didn't. She felt naughty and shameless and she sensed her face reddening, but not because of self-consciousness.

"You look so beautiful at the moment, your eyes heavy with desire, your cheeks rosy, plump lips parted with your panting breath. It's all I can do to stop myself from spreading you out on this table and taking you. Hard."

Her breath stuttered. She wanted that. She was way past caring about social niceties. In fact, she wouldn't have cared if Donovan had followed through with his threat.

"Are you wet?" he asked, licking his lips and staring at her nipples.

She nodded. "Yes, Sir."

He closed his eyes and dropped his head back, fisting his hands on the table. Makayla knew he was working to retain control, and the knowledge that it was she causing him to struggle so hard made her feel powerful and incredibly desirable.

"Good evening. I'm glad to see that you are still with us, Makayla."

She sat up, her gaze shooting to Fernando, who was suddenly standing by their table.

Fernando looked at her chest and licked his lips. Makayla colored, this time in embarrassment. She glanced down quickly. God, her nipples were like thumbtacks, clearly visible beneath the fabric of her dress and *jiggling*. Abruptly the vibrations ceased. Makayla looked toward Donovan, who glared daggers in Fernando's direction.

"I see that… How do you say…? You have kissed and made up?"

Donovan shifted in his seat, effectively shielding Makayla from Fernando's hungry gaze. "Yes," he responded stiffly. "Even though you've tried your best to keep that from happening."

Fernando arched an eyebrow. "You are mistaken, Mr. King. I merely assisted a lovely lady in distress. I couldn't allow her to make her way back to the hotel in such a state. It would have been very remiss of me."

"And you were there to save the day," Donovan snarled sarcastically.

Fernando ignored his comment and focused his attention on Makayla. "You are quite well, *querida*?"

Makayla felt Donovan stiffen beside her. "She is quite well, as you can see, Martínez."

She cast Donovan a side glance and noted his hard jaw and narrowed eyes. He clearly wasn't happy with the man.

"Yes, I do see," Fernando responded with a slight smile. "I'll leave you to enjoy the remainder of your meal. I hope to see you again soon, *señorita*." He gave a small bow and moved to talk to a couple nearby.

The waiter arrived and placed dessert menus in front of them. Donovan picked them up and gave them back to him, addressing the man in rapid Spanish. The waiter nodded and hurried away.

Makayla gave Donovan an enquiring look.

"I asked for something special," he explained. "It's not on the menu, but I've had it here before, and they're happy to accommodate their best clients."

"A surprise, then," she cried happily. Her thoughts drifted to Fernando as she studied him across the restaurant. "Fernando seems to be here quite a lot."

"He has rooms here. He shares his time between the hotel and the club," Donovan said dismissively.

Makayla returned her gaze to Donovan. "I thought he was a friend of yours?"

"He is, to a certain extent," he muttered. "As you know, we have some things in common and enjoy a similar lifestyle. That's about the extent of our friendship. We certainly haven't gone fishing together or to a game. Also, since we've arrived he's shown an...interest in you, which I don't appreciate. I think he's harboring a hope that I'll eventually revert to my old ways and ask you to participate in a threesome." He grimaced in distaste. "The thought appalls me. I'll never agree to such a thing with you."

"What if *I* wanted to experiment like that?" *There I go again, poking the bear.*

His jaw hardened and his eyes turned icy. "Are you interested in him like that, Makayla?" he asked, his voice ominously low.

"No, I'm just curious as to how you would react if it was something that I wanted."

He studied her coolly for a moment. "It's not something that I could bring myself to do. I definitely couldn't be involved. As you know, the thought of you with another man makes me feel violent, and I'd try everything to talk you out of it." He frowned. "Are you playing with me right now, baby? Trying to push my buttons? Because you're doing a fucking good job of it."

She supposed she was goading him, and she had no idea why she was doing it. Was she getting some kinky enjoyment out of his possessiveness? She thought deep down that she was. She had to admit that she liked his sense of ownership toward her. It made her feel safe and protected. She also recognized that she still felt vulnerable, and her self-confidence, while having increased tenfold since she'd met

Donovan, was still fragile. She suspected that she subconsciously sought validation of his feelings toward her. She was saved from voicing her thoughts, however, by the waiter's return. He placed a small pot on the table, lighting a gas flame underneath it then deposited a platter of fresh fruit between them. The scent of chocolate wafted up to tantalize her taste buds. She'd thought that she'd be unable to eat dessert, but that idea disappeared as she caught site of the oozing, chocolaty concoction bubbling away in the pot. The waiter handed them each a long, two-pronged fork then left them alone.

"Chocolate fondue," Donovan announced. "It's not Spanish, but Swiss, of course. It's a sensual dessert. Chocolate and fruit make a very heady combination."

Makayla smiled and leaned closer to him on their bench seat. "Another shared course, Mr. King," she murmured, licking her lips seductively.

Donovan growled, his words emerging in a husky rumble. "Yes, angel. I've decided, always shared meals with you."

He speared a segment of orange with his fork then swirled it through the chocolate, blowing on it softly before bringing it up to her mouth. She opened and he slipped the chocolaty fruit between her lips. The tang of orange and the richness of the cocoa combined to create a flavor so divine that she moaned in appreciation, closing her eyes to relish the taste on her tongue. She swallowed and opened her eyes as Donovan leaned forward and swiped chocolate from the side of her lips. He stared at her, his gaze smoldering, and sucked his finger into his mouth.

Makayla's belly clenched and she squeezed her thighs together. Donovan was right. The dessert was very sensual, erotic even, when eaten so seductively.

She repeated his actions, spearing a slice of banana and swirling it through the chocolate before feeding it to him. When the chocolate smeared across his lips, she bent toward him, lifting her body off the seat, and licked his lips, slowly and thoroughly. He groaned, a low rumble that she felt vibrate through her. She kissed him, slipping her tongue into his mouth and savoring the taste of fruit and chocolate.

He clutched her ass and yanked her harder into his side, grasping one of her thighs and sweeping it up so it rested across his lap. She should have felt embarrassed and inhibited by their environment, but all conscious thought fled her, leaving only the feel of Donovan's hard body pressed against hers and his demanding mouth as he kissed her passionately.

Suddenly, the vibrations started again, little pinpricks of sensation assaulting her nipples. She gasped into his mouth and he swallowed the sound with his kiss, massaging the cheeks of her ass and crushing her to him.

She was so drunk with lust, her mind felt like it was swimming through molasses. She slumped against him and wrapped her arms around his shoulders.

He swept one hand from her ass, over her hip to the inside of her thigh, his forefinger running up the sensitive skin until he reached the juncture of her legs. He ran his finger lightly over her curls then slipped it between the lips of her pussy, spreading her moisture around.

She groaned and broke their kiss, throwing her head back against the booth.

"You're so wet, baby," Donovan breathed against her neck, sliding his finger slowly in and out of her and nibbling her throat. "Always so wet and ready for me."

"Yes," she agreed, unable to stop her hips from thrusting up to meet his plunging finger. The vibration on her nipples sent little shock currents directly to her clit. *How are they connected?*

"We need to get out of here. Now," Donovan mumbled, his mouth pressed to her throat.

Chapter Twenty-Six

Donovan grasped Makayla's hand and tugged her behind him. He was heading toward the massage rooms. He'd organized it with Fernando earlier, and it was late, the massage therapists all having left for the day.

He unlocked the door and urged Makayla over the threshold, relocking it after them. The herbal scent of massage oil hung heavily in the air. He took a door to the right. He'd been down earlier and set up what he wanted. All the new toys he'd purchased were laid out neatly on a trolley.

"Get undressed," he instructed Makayla.

He watched as she untied the straps of her dress and shrugged the fabric off her shoulders to stand before him, naked. The soft glow of the mood lighting gave her body a beautiful luminosity. His breath hitched and he couldn't tear his gaze away. He stood still, drinking her in and relishing the way she squirmed under his scrutiny.

"Stay still," he ordered.

She stopped fidgeting immediately and lowered her eyes. Perfect, she was learning. He reached over and removed the vibrating pedant necklace. There'd be no need for that at the moment.

"Get onto the table, on hands and knees."

She climbed onto the massage table and took up the position he'd instructed, her pert ass bobbing in front of him. The table was larger and sturdier than the standard type. He needed the additional space for what he intended to do.

He tied a black scarf over her eyes. "I'm blindfolding you to heighten your awareness. With your sense of sight gone, it means you can better focus on what I'm doing to you," he explained. "It also adds a sense of anticipation and a little anxiety, not knowing what to expect next."

He picked up a locking wrist and ankle spreader bar and quickly affixed the bindings to her ankles.

"Rest on your chest and pass your arms between your legs," he ordered.

She did as he asked and he attached the bindings to her wrists, forcing her ass farther into the air. He tested the cuffs, ensuring that there was enough slack so as not to hurt her. The purpose of this scene was not to punish her but to push her a little, to open her eyes to new and different experiences that she could draw from in the future.

Her breathing increased, indicating that she was anxious. He placed his palm between her shoulder blades and smoothed it down her spine. "Relax, sweetheart. I'm not going to hurt you. This is a very different position than you're used to." He continued to stroke her back, encouraging a sense of calm to come over her. "It's intimidating because it leaves you wide open and vulnerable. You can't close your legs, nor can you move your arms. You're at my complete mercy, totally under my control. This is why trust between the Dominant and the submissive is so important, baby. You need to trust that I'm going to do the right thing by you and that I'll recognize your limitations. I know that you're anxious because I can hear the difference in your breathing. Also your pulse rate has increased. I felt it when I tested your bindings. And you're tense. Your muscles are taut with nervousness. These are things that a good Dominant will recognize and acknowledge."

He picked up the massage oil and squeezed some onto his palms, then he placed both his hands on her shoulders and started to rub, using his thumbs to dig into her tight muscles. Almost instantly, she started to relax.

"Understand that I'll *never* leave you like this. I. Will. *Never*. Leave. You. Alone—in bindings." He dug his thumbs in hard after each word to emphasize his point. "Also, remember your safe word. You say that word at any time you feel you can't continue. Do you understand?"

"Yes, Sir." Her voice was strong and steady, giving him the assurance that he needed to continue.

He selected a tube of lubricant and squirted some between her ass cheeks, using his fingers to spread it around her backside. He progressed slowly, not wanting to startle her with any sudden movements. Gradually, he worked his fingers closer to her anus, brushing them over her tight little sphincter before he plunged a finger, knuckle deep, inside.

She gasped and stiffened.

"Shh," he soothed. "Relax, baby." He worked the one finger in and out of her asshole, going deeper each time and stretching her tight little channel. Her muscles lost their rigidity, and her sphincter relaxed around his thrusting. That's what he needed—for her to relax fully and give herself completely to him. He squirted more lube and used a second finger, gradually stretching and manipulating her anus. Fuck, he was so turned on it was taking all of his willpower to maintain the slow and steady pace he'd promised he'd use with her. Under his ministrations, her sphincter was stretching, the hole gradually widening.

She quivered and he looked at her face, her head resting on one cheek—her lips were slightly parted, her breathing choppy, a rosy flush suffusing her features.

"Are you okay, baby?" His voice was gruff with his own need.

"Yes," she whispered. "It feels different…but good."

"Excellent." He reached for the butt plug that he'd purchased earlier that day. It was small and designed for people new to anal play. He squeezed lube onto the plug then pressed it against Makayla's sphincter, pushing past the tight muscles until it was nestled fully in her anus. Then he switched it on, the little vibrations breaking the silence of the room.

She jumped and whimpered. He smoothed his palm over her ass cheeks, willing her to relax until gradually her body loosened and her breathing steadied.

"That's it, baby. Well done."

He stood back and looked at her. She was so fucking beautiful, bound and blindfolded and totally open to him, completely at his mercy, the butt plug nestled flush against the cheeks of her ass. She jutted her backside out and she tried to rub her pussy against her arms, attempting to seek some relief. Her cunt was wet with arousal, the blonde curls glistening in the candlelight. Fuck, she was really turned on.

He toed his shoes off, removed his socks and shrugged out of his shirt. He'd planned on drawing the play out longer, but he couldn't contain himself. He needed to be inside her.

He undid the zipper on his pants, shoved them down his legs and tossed them aside. He reached inside his boxers and grasped his aching cock. He was so hard it was painful. He fisted his erection roughly and relished the sight of Makayla laid out and open before him in perfectly bound submission. Pre-cum gathered on his tip and he used it to lubricate his shaft, pumping his fist slowly along his length, drawing out the anticipation.

Makayla whimpered and wriggled.

"I'm still here," he barked. "Stop moving."

She lay motionless once again, immediately following his orders. Fuck, she was going to make a perfect submissive. She did everything he asked without question, trusting him implicitly. He just had to ensure that he wouldn't ever give her reason to doubt him.

He knew she was desperately aroused. The vibrations from the butt plug were relentless and her inability to move would be driving her crazy. She couldn't close her legs to get that relief he knew she'd be craving.

He held out, continuing to stare at her and drawing out the tension, squeezing his cock hard to control his own arousal.

Lubricant trickled out of her asshole, and she was so wet a bead of moisture dripped out of her pussy to splash on the tabletop.

"Fuck! That is so hot." He groaned and yanked on his cock. He couldn't wait any longer. He needed inside her—now. He climbed onto the table behind her, grasped her hips and thrust into her, hard, stilling when he felt himself hit her deep inside, his balls smacking against her clit.

She yelped, tightened her pussy then relaxed around him. The vibrations from the butt plug coursed through his cock. The feeling was indescribable and he knew wasn't going to last long.

He drew back and drove into her, pushing her body up the table with the force of his thrusts. Her pussy was wet, hot and clenched around his shaft like a fist, the butt plug making her tighter. He growled and pumped harder, rutting into her like a wild beast. Sweat gathered on his brow and his muscles tightened as he fought to maintain control. Then he felt it, that glorious sensation of fluttering turned to throbbing, then to long, drawn-out pulses as Makayla climaxed all over his cock. She whimpered and moaned and made little humping movements beneath him, riding out her orgasm.

He roared her name, lost in the delirium of his impending release, and grasped her hips harder, his fingers digging into her tender flesh. He bucked, gyrated his hips and thrust deeply, feeling her cervix as he hit the back of her and emptied his seed in long, euphoric bursts.

Chapter Twenty-Seven

Makayla lay panting and spent, too exhausted to move, even if it had been possible. Donovan rested lightly on her back, his heaving breaths hot and heavy in her ear.

Slowly he lifted himself off her. The vibrations in her ass had stopped and she felt him unclasp the cuffs at her wrists and ankles then her blindfold was removed. She blinked, letting her eyesight adjust to the soft candlelight of the room.

Donovan sat on the table and pulled her onto his lap, massaging her limbs and working the stiffness out.

"How do you feel?" he murmured.

"Hmm, good, very good."

He chuckled. "You did really well, baby. You're a natural." His voice held an undercurrent of praise. "Not many people would have adjusted so quickly to the spreader bar."

"Is that what those things are called?" She'd wondered but had forgotten to ask.

"Well, strictly speaking, this one is called a locking wrist and ankle spreader bar. It's better for what I wanted to do with you." He continued to massage life into her limbs. "How did you like the butt plug?"

She blushed at the thought of what an eyeful Donovan would have had. Her position hadn't allowed for any modesty, and the recollection of him fingering her most private of places had her face flaming. "I liked it," she finally whispered, knowing that he needed an answer from her.

He tightened his arms around her. "Good, I'm glad." He dropped a kiss to the top of her head. "Anal play is very erotic, if both partners enjoy it."

He stood and dropped her to her feet, then he strolled over to an armoire and removed two fluffy white robes. "We can go back to our suite dressed in these."

She looked down at the massage table. "What about the table? It's a mess."

"I'll collect the toys and wipe it down later. The cleaners come in every morning and disinfect everything."

He grabbed her hand. "Come, it's late. I need to put you in bed."

* * * *

Makayla slept well but woke up feeling stiff and sore. She was aching in places where she hadn't even known that she had muscles. She stretched, and groaned as the movement caused her discomfort.

"I've run a bath," Donovan informed her as he strode into their bedroom dressed in nothing but tight white Calvin Klein boxers. Makayla allowed her gaze to travel over his powerful body, stopping to drink in the defined V on his abdomen.

"I daresay that you're stiff this morning."

"Yes," she agreed, struggling to sit up comfortably.

"It will get easier as you become accustomed to the range of positions and activities." He bent, swept her up into his arms and headed for the bathroom. "I've put Epsom salts in the bath. It will help with your muscle stiffness."

He reached the bathtub and lowered her into it, then he kicked off his boxers before he stepped in to settle his body behind hers. He picked up the washcloth and stroked it over her shoulders and cleavage, running it in circles up her throat and across her clavicle. She sighed in pleasure and relaxed into him, feeling the soreness in her limbs starting to melt away.

They lay in silence for some minutes, each deep in their own thoughts. Makayla thought about Infierno and Donovan's position there. She wanted to go back to the club, but this time she wanted to be there as Donovan's submissive.

"Will you take me to Infierno tonight?" she asked quietly. She wasn't sure what his reaction would be, as they hadn't actually discussed going to the club together.

He stiffened then stilled for a moment before recommencing his soothing caresses. "I don't think that's a good idea," he eventually responded.

She sighed. "Why not? Why won't you take me there?"

"Because you're new to this. You're still in training."

"Don't other people still in training go to the club? Isn't that how they learn?"

He huffed out a breath. "Yes, but you're not other people. You're mine, and I'm not sure that I'd deal well with other men watching you."

She turned and straddled his lap, throwing her arms around his neck. "Pleeease. I think it's important. I want to experience everything and *you* obviously enjoy going to clubs."

He gave her a level look and brushed some stray curls from her forehead. "I suppose we can try it," he finally conceded. "It is an opportunity for you to observe some scenes. But you have to do everything that I tell you. I won't have you wandering off by yourself. The Dominants there, for the most part, are responsible and won't approach a submissive they know belongs to someone else." He shrugged. "But there are some who are new to the club or the scene who won't necessarily follow the rules."

She bounced up and down on his lap, sending water sloshing over the edge of the tub. "I'll do anything you tell me," she promised. She felt his hard length pressed against the inside of her thigh.

"Careful of the goods, baby." He grimaced. "I'm hard but I won't be touching you this morning, you need time to recover. I fucked you hard last night."

She giggled. "You did, and you *are* the one who insists on delayed gratification." She adjusted her position on his lap so as not to make him uncomfortable. "Can we go shopping today? I want to buy an outfit like the ones I saw the women wearing at Infierno."

He looked at her in horror. "You are not dressing in flimsy, barely-there clothes."

"Everyone else does." She scowled at him. "I'll stand out terribly if you don't let me dress appropriately."

He dropped his head back to rest on the edge of the tub and closed his eyes. Makayla waited with bated breath. She was prepared to argue this point. She knew that she was supposed to be doing what Donovan ordered in relation to these issues, but she didn't want to be conspicuous *and* she wanted him to relax his stance on her wardrobe.

Finally, he raised his head and looked at her. "Fine," he said tersely. "But I get the final say."

Makayla grinned, happy that she hadn't needed to push the issue. She was excited about going to Infierno, she wanted to observe the BDSM scenes and play, but this time she'd be with Donovan and not feeling like an interloper, as she had when she'd followed him that night. Another part of her wanted to stamp her ownership on Donovan. She wanted to show the other submissives that he was no longer available to them. At least, that's what she expected, but she realized suddenly that they hadn't discussed it.

She gave him a serious look. "Donovan, you don't want to play with other submissives, do you? While you're with me?" She held her breath, waiting for his answer.

His eyes widened. "Of course not." He looked at her intently. "Only you, baby. The only reason that I was dominating that other submissive was because I needed the release and I wanted to ensure that my willpower and my self-discipline hadn't completely deserted me. I told you that. I admit it was a serious error in judgment on my part, but I had no other mechanism for dealing with all the foreign emotions I was feeling."

She leaned forward and placed a soft kiss on his lips, relief coursing through her. He grasped her backside and tugged her tighter to him, rubbing his hard cock between the lips of her pussy. She moaned into his mouth and he chuckled.

"Don't get too comfortable," he mumbled against her lips. "We need to get organized if you want to hit the shops."

Chapter Twenty-Eight

A fierce fluttering sensation had taken root in Makayla's belly and her hands felt clammy. She took deep breaths, willing her heart rate to calm.

She studied her reflection in the mirror, still dismayed at the difference in her appearance. She wore black, skintight leather pants that had taken her an age to wriggle into. Her latex halter-neck plunged low in the front and gripped her breasts like two firm hands, sending her cleavage spilling over the top. The back of the halter-neck dipped to tie in a short corset style, low on her spine. She sported sky-high platform heels in scarlet red, the same shade as her lipstick. She'd tied her thick blonde hair into a high plait, the end hitting just below her bare shoulder blades. In truth, she felt that she looked more like a Dominatrix than a submissive. She cocked her head to one side and assessed her image.

"You look...gorgeous," a deep voice said from behind her. "Like fucking sex personified!"

She turned to face Donovan and his gaze raked her body from head to toe.

"That outfit should be illegal," he whispered, stepping closer to her.

She frowned. "I was just thinking that I look like a Dominatrix."

Donovan produced a box from his inside pocket. "That's why you'll be wearing this." He opened the box, removed a necklace and turned her so that she was once more facing the mirror. He placed the necklace around her and locked it in place with a soft click. It sat high on her throat, like a choker, thick and smooth, the links fastened closely together in a snake chain. A ring encircled the chain to sit snugly at the base of her throat. She caressed the cold metal in admiration.

Donovan stood behind her, a hand on each of her shoulders. Her heels made her taller, her head reaching to his chin. He bent a little to speak in her ear. "It's platinum and it signifies that you belong to me." He met her eyes in the mirror. "Did you read about being collared, baby?"

She nodded, mesmerized and rendered silent by his intense gaze.

"It means that no one else may touch you without my permission. There are a number of different types of collar, and strictly speaking, as a novice submissive, you should have a training collar. But these things can be done differently—the wearing of the collar and how it's worn is up to the Dominant, and I need everyone to know that you're mine, and as such, untouchable. Do you agree?"

"Yes, Sir."

"Good. At the moment, you're able to take it off, I haven't locked it into place. That won't happen until we're both ready. You need to be certain that it's what you want and I need to be certain that you're ready."

At the mention of collars and submissive behavior, Makayla had bowed her head, reminded from her brief study of the lifestyle that she shouldn't look directly at Donovan.

He hooked her chin with his index finger and tipped her head up so that she was once more meeting his gaze in the mirror. "I like your subservient attitude, baby. But I need you to look at me when I talk about this issue. It's important that you understand and I need to be sure that you're in agreement."

"I understand, Sir," she murmured, suddenly overwhelmed by the magnitude of their situation, but also turned on by the fact that Donovan had collared her. It was a heady feeling, knowing that she belonged to someone as dominant and powerfully masculine as Donovan. "I like the collar, Sir. Very much."

He gave her a devilish smile. "That's good, angel. You've made me very happy." He looked at his watch. "It's nine-thirty, so we should leave." He retrieved a light coat from the foot of the bed. "Wear this until we reach the club."

* * * *

Donovan stepped inside Infierno with Makayla tucked tightly under his arm.

Carlos greeted him from behind the desk. "*El Rey. Buenas noches.*"

Donovan nodded curtly and made his way behind the curtain. He still hadn't gotten over the fact that Carlos had basically announced to Makayla who and what he was. It hadn't been the doorman's fault entirely. He hadn't known who Makayla was and had probably assumed that she was just another woman looking to learn from The King of Infierno. But the prudent thing would have been for Carlos to have found him before allowing her to waltz into the club unannounced.

He tugged Makayla in behind him, keeping a tight hold on her hand. All chatter ceased as they appeared at the entrance to the bar area, and people turned their heads to stare. Makayla shrank beside him at the attention they were receiving. He pulled her close and dropped his mouth to her head, speaking into her hair.

"They're curious, baby. They've never seen me bring anyone here before."

"*Rey*." Various men nodded in greeting, their gazes darting over Makayla inquisitively.

Donovan nodded curtly in response, winding his way through the tables and chairs.

"There's a dressing room and bathroom in there." He pointed to the right. "Freshen up, remove your jacket and meet me back here. Don't go anywhere else."

She nodded meekly, dropped his hand and headed in the direction he'd indicated. He sighed and shoved a hand through his hair. This was going to be harder than he'd initially anticipated. He didn't need to change, since he'd dressed in black pants and a white cotton, collarless shirt. He rolled his sleeves to his elbows and paced up and down, waiting for Makayla to reappear.

She returned some minutes later, and his heart stuttered in his chest. Christ, she was so fucking hot. Those leather pants and the sky-high fuck-me heels made her legs seem a mile long. Her breasts spilled enticingly over her top, her cleavage smooth and plump, giving him the sudden urge to shove his head between her tits. His collar sparkled clearly and brightly around her neck. He glanced over his shoulder to the bar area, where once again everything had stopped and all eyes were on Makayla.

He was standing in front of her in two strides. He pulled her close and glared around, a fierce possessiveness taking hold of him. He was glad he'd thought to collar her before they came. It meant that there was no doubt that she was taken. He took her hand in his and headed toward one of the play areas. He wanted her to observe and take note of the things the Dom did and how the sub responded.

He stopped in front of a St. Andrew's Cross. A woman, bound with her back to the apparatus stood naked except for a tiny pair of panties and nipple clamps. She wore a black blindfold and gag, her head bowed as she waited for her Dom.

Donovan positioned Makayla in front of him. "Kneel," he instructed, pushing gently on her shoulders. She stiffened and looked around at him, her eyes wide. He needed her to understand that in the club it was expected that a submissive acted as such and should always obey his or her Dom without question. He could stretch the guidelines, of course, it wasn't written in stone. He wanted her to understand the entire experience and to appreciate the practice of being a submissive.

He arched an eyebrow at her. "Are you defying me?"

She shook her head and sank slowly to her knees. "No, Sir."

He widened his stance, his legs on the outside of hers, and nestled the back of her head at his crotch. Not the best position for maintaining his self-control, but Makayla would feel him behind her and be reassured by his physical presence. He placed his hands on her shoulders and her body started to loosen under his touch. He rubbed his thumbs along the column of her throat and she moaned quietly. Good, she was calm and relaxed. Now that she'd accepted her position, he'd sit. He caught the eye of a staff member and motioned his head toward a chair. A moment later, a comfortable-looking armchair was positioned at his side. He sat and pulled Makayla's braid, directing her body backward until she was pressed against his left thigh.

The crowd quieted as a tall, lean man stepped into the circle of light and strode toward the St. Andrew's Cross.

Donovan bent his head and spoke quietly to Makayla. "The man's name is Manuel Sanchez. He's a good Dom, adept at reading his sub's needs."

It would be good for Makayla to watch this particular scene.

The bound woman lifted her head subtly, aware of the approach of her Dom. He circled her, whip in hand, and tested her restraints, pulling on the nipple clamps until she groaned and shuddered. He ran the whip handle across her cleavage, around each of her breasts and down her torso, stopping at the juncture of her thighs. He rubbed the handle over her pussy, massaging her over the fabric of her panties. She pulled on her bindings and moaned, the sound muffled through her gag.

Suddenly Manuel drew the whip back and sent it cracking through the air to land across her torso, following it with a second rapid flick of his wrist, landing the whip just above the first lash.

Makayla stiffened beside him. He placed his palm on her head and caressed her hair soothingly until she relaxed once more.

Manuel started a rapid flow of lashes placed strategically over the sub's body, not any one striking the same piece of flesh twice. Donovan could tell that he was skilled in the use of the whip, wielding the device with expert precision. His sub groaned, but Donovan could tell that her breathing was even, her hands steady and relaxed in the bindings, indicating that she wasn't thinking of using hand signals to convey her safe word. And Manuel watched her intently, gauging the strength of his lashes to his sub's physical cues, knowing when to back off and when to make the next strike a little harder.

Donovan leaned down and spoke softly in Makayla's ear, explaining the Dom's approach and the sub's response to him.

The Dom finally dropped the whip, his chest glistening with perspiration, his breathing hard. He bent and released a nipple clamp then gently sucked the taut peak into his mouth. The sub arched in her restraints, her mouth wide around her gag.

"When the pressure is released, blood rushes to the nipple and the pain is intense for a moment. Her Dom is sucking and licking her to ease her discomfort," Donovan told Makayla quietly. He gazed at her profile and was gratified to see that she seemed aroused by what she was witnessing. Her face flushed a rosy pink and her chest heaved slightly from her increased breathing. "See how the sub has relaxed already?" he continued. "The initial bite of pain has gone and Manuel is being careful to be gentle with her nipples. He knows they'll be very sensitive."

Makayla squirmed and gripped his thigh, her nails biting into his flesh through his pants.

"Do you like what you see, baby?"

"Yes, Sir," she murmured. "I'd like you to do that to me."

"Look at me," he demanded. She turned her head toward him, her violet eyes wide and glazed with desire. "Would you like to be on display for all to see, wearing nothing but your panties?"

She lowered her eyes. "Yes, Sir."

Fuck, he'd asked her to be honest, but he didn't like her answer—at all. He fisted his hands on the armrest and ground his teeth together. He wouldn't be able to cope with that. Perhaps he could reason with her, offer her a compromise.

"What if I, as your Dom, don't want you displayed like that?"

She looked up. "I would only do what you wanted, Sir."

"Good answer. We'll discuss it later." He marveled at how quickly she was falling into the submissive frame of mind. He suspected the club was helping with that. She was taking her cues from the other submissives and the BDSM environment was stimulating to say the least. To a novice like Makayla, it was like stepping into another world. People in training often felt the change come over them just by walking into a club.

The observers of Manuel's scene started drifting away, speaking quietly among themselves. The Dom, having released his sub, was striding with her in his arms to a quiet corner.

"He will look after her now," Donovan explained. "Aftercare of the submissive by the Dom is very important."

Donovan stood and tugged lightly on Makayla's braid, encouraging her to stand with him. She rose gracefully and stopped beside him. He traced his index finger along her cleavage, enjoying the feel of her soft skin.

A shadow fell over them, and he looked up and into familiar brown eyes.

"Well, well, *El Rey* is back." He'd recognize her accent anywhere, a cross between Spanish and French that he'd once found immensely sexy.

"Dolores." He nodded curtly and attempted to sidestep her, gripping Makayla's hand tightly.

But Dolores wasn't finished with him. "You know I prefer Lola." Her lips curled into a sly smile. "Is that any way to treat your ex?"

Chapter Twenty-Nine

Makayla stood frozen to the spot. Where had this woman come from? And what did she want with Donovan? Makayla glanced across at Donovan, who was scowling at the woman, his hand tightening around Makayla's own. Makayla's attention returned to the beauty standing in front of them. She had an exotic look with high cheekbones, caramel-colored eyes and long, silky black hair. And she wore the most outrageously skimpy outfit that Makayla could never imagine being worn outside a bedroom. She may as well have been walking around in the nude — that wasn't too outrageous given their environment. But there was something about her ensemble that covered — though not entirely — her private parts, which made it look more obscene. The corset she wore had cutouts around her nipples, making the pointed tips all the more prominent and drawing the eye to the turgid peaks. Her pierced nipples sported gold rings, and from them dangled a string of beads. The corset ended just above a pair of brief panties that displayed more than they covered.

Makayla blushed and focused her attention on the carpet. The situation was awkward to say the least and making it worse was the fact that Donovan hadn't said anything to disabuse her of the things that this Dolores — or Lola, or whatever her name was — was saying. Obviously, she *was* Donovan's ex-something, probably his ex-submissive, which wasn't surprising. He'd already admitted that he'd had a couple of serious relationships, it was just that this woman was so obviously experienced in the BDSM lifestyle, and beautiful with it and, when combined, it all just added to Makayla's insecurities.

As if sensing that his presence was required, Fernando suddenly appeared at their side. "Makayla," he murmured, picking up her hand and kissing the back. He turned his attention to Dolores. "Lola, it's been a while." He nodded at the other woman.

"Hello, Fernando," she purred.

Fernando looked at Donovan. "Perhaps you need a moment with Lola. I'll keep Makayla company."

Donovan glared at the man, his jaw tight with tension, but he didn't object as Fernando led her away.

Fernando settled them into seats at the bar then left to order. Makayla studied him as he chatted to the bartender. He wore black leather pants and a billowy black shirt. It was so odd to see him in anything but his conservative suits and ties that a spontaneous giggle erupted from her.

"What are you laughing about?" Fernando asked, having returned with their wine.

"Nothing," she assured him, not wanting him to think she was laughing at him. She took a sip of wine, her gaze wandering to where they'd left Donovan speaking to Dolores, but she could no longer see them. "Who was that woman?"

Fernando sighed. "You should ask Donovan that question, Makayla. It is not for me to talk about."

Makayla huffed out a breath in frustration. "She said that she was his ex."

Fernando hummed noncommittally and it was clear that he wasn't going to comment any further.

She glanced around once more, searching for Donovan, but she couldn't see him. *Where have they gone?* She suddenly felt awkward, out of place and irritated. Donovan had made it clear that she wasn't to leave his side, but it seemed okay for *him* to leave her.

"Perhaps I should go back to the hotel," she murmured.

Fernando eyed her over the top of his glass. "Do you think that's wise?"

She shrugged. "I don't know where Donovan's gone, but obviously Delores needed to speak with him about something private."

Fernando sighed and placed his glass on the table. "If you are so set on leaving, I will come with you. Of course, I risk life and limb by taking you away from here. *El Rey* will not be happy." He gave a pointed look at her necklace. "He has you collared, which means I will be breaking one of the cardinal rules—interfering with another Dom's sub."

"I'll tell him that I insisted on leaving," she assured him.

He stood and held his hand out for her. "You should know that defying your Dom will have dire consequences. I appreciate you are new to the lifestyle, but you understand that much, yes?"

He rested his hand at her elbow and guided her toward the door.

"I understand," she confirmed. "But he said that he wouldn't leave me alone and made me promise to stay by *his* side."

"But you weren't alone. I was with you. He never would have left you had I not been there. Are you doing this to punish him?"

She couldn't put her finger on exactly why she was so determined to leave, but running into Donovan's ex had made her feel incredibly awkward, and oddly, like she was an interloper. As if she was somewhere playing at something that she shouldn't be. Everyone in the club would know that Makayla was a novice and inexperienced in the scene and they'd also know that Dolores wasn't.

Makayla shook her head. "I just don't feel comfortable."

"Very well. Collect your belongings while I hail us a taxi."

* * * *

Donovan stalked toward the bar. He hadn't seen Lola in two years and she turned up the very night that he was initiating Makayla into the club lifestyle. She'd sought him out under the guise of giving him a message from his parents, but he knew that her intention was to make a nuisance of herself in front of his new sub. And what the hell was she doing visiting his parents anyway? It would just send them the wrong message.

He stood at the entry to the bar area and scanned the crowd. There was no sign of Makayla. He pushed a hand through his hair and squared his jaw. "Where is the woman I was with?" he asked the bartender.

"She left with Martínez."

"What the fuck?" Donovan snarled, impotent rage coursing through his veins. The man obviously had a death wish. How dare he leave with Donovan's submissive!

Donovan stalked to the exit and hailed a cab, jumping in quickly and barking directions to the driver. He looked at his watch. He'd been waylaid by Dolores for over thirty minutes. He should have just ignored her and not have given her the satisfaction of his attention.

What the hell was Makayla thinking by leaving with Martínez? She'd know that Donovan would be pissed off. Was she testing him? She'd better hope that her backside had recovered from her spanking because she was just about to experience what a real punishment was all about. He had that unreasonable fear again, clenching his gut. He knew it was crazy, but that was what she did to him, making him even angrier at her thoughtlessness.

Finally, they pulled up in front of the hotel. He paid the driver and strode into the lobby. It was late but there were still groups of people milling around the foyer, laughing and drinking. He spied Makayla sitting with Fernando. He stalked over to them, his jaw tight with tension, but the fear clenching his gut had started to abate as soon as he caught sight of her. He grasped Makayla under the arms and hauled her to her feet.

"Donovan," she breathed in surprise. "You startled me."

Donovan cupped the nape of her neck and turned her toward the elevators. He shot a glare over his shoulder at Fernando. "I'll talk to *you* later!"

"Fernando wanted me to stay, but I was insistent on leaving," she babbled.

He ignored her and started walking in the direction of the elevator bank, keeping his hand firmly on her neck.

"Please, I'm sorry. I just felt uncomfortable and I didn't know where you'd gone."

He punched in the code for the elevator and urged Makayla forward, stepping inside after her.

Donovan could see the anxiety etched across her face and it pleased him immensely. Good, she was nervous.

"What are you going to do?" she asked, a slight tremor in her voice.

"I'm going to punish you, of course. What did you expect?" He gave her a hard look. "Did you leave to test me, Makayla?"

"No. I told you I was uncomfortable after your ex showed up."

"That's exactly what she is, an *ex*," he snarled. "She has nothing to do with us. In fact, that's the first time I've seen her in two years."

They arrived at their suite. Donovan unlocked the door, urging Makayla onward.

"Go into the bedroom. Get undressed and kneel by the end of the bed."

She scurried to do his bidding and disappeared behind the bedroom door. He wandered over to the iPod docking station and selected *Sacrifice* by Aghast. It was music to suit his mood—sinister. He took a couple of deep breaths. He shouldn't have touched her in anger. He needed to be in total control of his emotions and his actions. When he'd realized that she was safe and he had her back, he'd felt a great wave of relief wash through him. He was still furious, but his fear had left him. He waited for five minutes, quieting his breathing and drawing out Makayla's anxiety.

When he felt calm enough, he entered the bedroom. She was kneeling on the floor at the foot of the bed, her hair loose and flowing around her bowed head, her beautiful skin bare and glowing softly from the illumination of the bedside lamp. She stiffened when she noticed him enter the room.

"You know that I was scared for you," he said, his voice resonating deeply. It was his Dom's voice. "What you did, leaving like that, was thoughtless and disobedient."

"I'm sorry, Sir," she whispered.

"And you left with another Dom, of all people. You're *mine*! You don't leave a premises in the company of another Dom without my permission!"

She jumped, startled at his harsh tone.

He strode over to the dresser and removed what he required. The music's tempo built around them, haunting voices now adding to the dark beat. He watched as a shiver rippled down Makayla's spine. She was affected – that was good.

He stood behind her quietly, drawing out her unease. He wanted her off balance, and he needed her to realize that what she'd done was not acceptable. Even outside a D/s relationship, it was thoughtless to up and leave your partner without a word, particularly in an unfamiliar country.

Finally, he leaned forward, bending at the waist. "Stand up." He spoke softly into her ear.

She wobbled to her feet. He grasped her shoulders and spun her around to face him. Picking up the nipple clamps that he'd retrieved from the dresser, he held them up in front of her face. They weren't harsh – he'd selected them specifically because they were for novices and he hadn't wanted to hurt her but get her accustomed to the use of such devices. The tweezer clamps were perfect for that.

He bent and sucked a nipple into his mouth, drawing hard on the taut bud until she moaned and swayed toward him. He released it with a pop and fixed a clamp to the turgid peak.

"Is that bearable?" he asked, tightening the clamp until she gasped.

"Yes, Sir."

He nodded and sucked her other nipple into his mouth, using his tongue to caress the peak to its maximum tautness before affixing the clamp. He pulled on the chain connecting the clamps, and she moaned.

"You can use your safe word, but remember that this is also a punishment. Now lie across the end of the bed on your stomach."

She did as he had asked and he grasped her ankles, pulling her toward him until her feet touched the floor. He pushed a pillow under her belly to raise her ass in the air so just the tips of her toes were touching the carpet.

He picked up a paddle. He'd decided on the paddle as the best instrument for a beginner. The last thing he wanted to do was scare her to death, and the paddle wasn't as harsh as a whip or crop.

"Do you trust me?" he asked before he started.

She nodded. "Yes, Sir."

"Good, I'm going to give you fifteen strikes. Do you understand?"

"Yes, Sir."

"I want you to count."

She gripped the bed covers and pushed her face into the mattress.

He pulled his hand back and sent the paddle whipping through the air to land on her ass.

She jumped and yelped. "One," she muttered.

He sent the paddle flying a second time, but was careful to strike her ass in a different spot.

"Two," she yelled into the mattress.

Her knuckles were white where she gripped the bedcovers, but otherwise, she looked calm enough. After all, he hadn't even bound her, so there was nothing stopping her from jumping up and running off. He'd deliberately left it like that to give her some sense of control. It was the first time he'd used an instrument on her and he wanted her to feel safe with it.

He struck her a third time and she moaned low in her throat and pushed her ass higher in the air. The fourth smack he aimed between her thighs and she shuddered, barely able to mutter the number.

He stopped and ran his fingers between her legs, caressing her pussy lips, and was surprised and delighted to see that she was turned on. *Fuck.* She was wet and swollen. This obviously wasn't going to be the punishment that he'd intended. He'd finish paddling her, but he'd have to do something else to exert discipline. He shifted uncomfortably, his erection huge, aching and pressing against his pants painfully.

He planted four more strikes on her backside, swiftly and surely, until her ass was a beautiful shade of pink. He pulled back and gave her a minute of respite before finishing her punishment.

Finally, he caressed his hand over her backside, gripping the two cheeks and squeezing. She let out a soft sigh and turned her head to the side, her eyelids heavy with lust and exhaustion.

"Sit up," he ordered.

She sat up and he feasted on her swaying breasts, the nipple clamps still firmly attached. He unsnapped one clamp and she gasped as the blood rushed to her nipple. He bent quickly and sucked it into his mouth, gently caressing the tortured peak. He repeated the process with her other nipple then urged her back down on the bed on her stomach, readjusting the pillow under her belly to raise her ass farther in the air.

Donovan unzipped his pants and released his turgid cock. He was so hard it physically pained him.

"I'm going to take you now, but I don't want you to come. This is part of your punishment."

He positioned himself behind her on the bed, his legs on the outside of hers, and thrust forward, hard. She groaned and forced herself back onto him, meeting his momentum with her own. He set a punishing rhythm, pulling back and plunging again and again, filling her tight little channel with his thick shaft, stretching her so she gripped him firmly. Fuck, but she was compact, and he worried that he'd hurt her, but her soft moans and little grunts of pleasure told him differently. He felt her fluttering deep in her core and he knew she was close to disobeying him again. She was still too new to the pleasure to control her reactions.

"Don't come," he muttered through clenched teeth. He lunged forward twice more, gripped her hips and climaxed hard, filling her with his cum and roaring a garbled version of her name.

Chapter Thirty

Makayla rubbed her backside. It was still a little tender, but nothing too unbearable. What had been truly unbearable was Donovan not allowing her to climax. She'd slept fitfully, glaring at his slumbering form and imagining different forms of torture she could inflict on him. The unresolved ache in her belly made her fractious and short-tempered.

She'd eventually decided a workout would be good for her and allow her to release some tension. Donovan had left early that morning for another meeting with real estate agents, so she had time to kill.

She dressed in her workout gear and headed to the gym. It was quiet and she had the place to herself. She jumped on the treadmill and jogged for ten minutes then transferred to the cross trainer for another ten minutes before grabbing a floor mat and finishing with half an hour of yoga.

She'd worked up a good sweat and released some tension and she was looking forward to a shower. She unlocked the door to their suite and walked inside, stopping dead in her tracks when she saw a woman relaxing on the lounge.

"Who are you?" Makayla asked, her voice tight with anxiety.

The woman stood and turned around—Dolores. Makayla gasped. "What do you want and how did you get in here?"

Dolores smiled. "I'm on Donovan's list of approved guests, of course."

Makayla's head was spinning. Why would Donovan have his ex on his list of guests?

As if she'd asked the question aloud, Dolores spoke. "Donovan has...needs."

"Well, I'd appreciate it if you left," Makayla responded, her voice sure and steady. "You're not welcome here, and I can meet any needs that he may have."

"Of course, *you're* not welcoming," Dolores purred. "But Donovan will be. I was his submissive for quite a while, you know. I let him do anything to me, and he told me that I was the best sub he ever had." She looked Makayla up and down, a sneer crossing her pretty features. "And I hear that you're new to the scene. I don't want to burst your bubble, but Donovan likes his subs to have experience. He won't want to waste time training someone for long, you know. Particularly someone so..." She gave Makayla another once-over, her gaze turning hard and flinty. "Someone so mousy and little."

Makayla stared at Dolores. She was hitting on the things that Makayla herself had thought, correctly identifying all of Makayla's insecurities. To make matters worse, Dolores looked beautiful and groomed to perfection. Her long black hair fell in a silky smooth veil down her back and she wore an elegant cream linen pantsuit and nude high heels. She looked cool and sophisticated. Her accent was also sexy, even Makayla had to acknowledge that. Next to her, Makayla felt disheveled, messy and very ordinary. She fidgeted awkwardly then decided that she needed to be strong and not let this harlot walk all over her.

She squared her shoulders and motioned to the door. "If Donovan wants you, Dolores, I'm sure he'll call. Until then, you can leave."

"Don't think you can get rid of me that easily," she snarled, the venom in her voice and demeanor turning her ugly. "There are things that he hasn't told you. He'll take me back, just you wait and see. We had something special and that sort of relationship doesn't happen overnight, nor does it just finish. We share a history."

Before Makayla could answer, the door to their suite opened and Donovan strolled in. He took in the scene quickly, his jaw tightening as he stared hard at Dolores. "What are you doing here?" he snapped.

Dolores pasted a smile onto her perfectly made-up face. "Donovan, darling. I dropped by to see you, of course. Your new little submissive and I were just chatting."

Makayla crossed her arms and glared at her. She'd hardly describe what they'd been doing as chatting. Chatting implied friendly banter, not the exchange of barbed comments.

Donovan grasped Dolores by the elbow and steered her toward the door. "I told you last night that I don't want to see you. Don't come back, Dolores, and leave Makayla alone. I don't want you anywhere near her, do you understand?"

Dolores nodded. "Of course, Sir. I'm sorry," she whispered obediently and allowed herself to be manhandled over the threshold of the suite.

Makayla stiffened. Those subservient words coming out of that woman's mouth sent a cold shudder through her, reminding her just what Donovan and Dolores had shared.

Finally, the awful woman had been removed.

"I'm going to have a shower," she muttered, and took herself off to the bathroom.

Makayla stood under the spray. She washed and conditioned her hair, feeling the tension slowly starting to seep from her shoulders. She was glad that Donovan had left her to shower in peace because she wanted the time to gather her thoughts. It was obvious that Dolores wanted Donovan back. What was not so obvious was what their history entailed. Dolores had certainly suggested that Makayla didn't know everything and that there were things that Donovan was keeping from her.

She stayed in the shower longer than necessary, shaving her legs and underarms and tidying up her bikini line. She'd decided that she was going to try a Brazilian wax. There was a spa on the second floor of the hotel and she'd made an appointment for the following morning. She was going to surprise Donovan and she hoped he'd be happy with the change.

She shut off the shower and toweled herself dry, wrapping her hair in an additional towel. She rubbed her body all over with lotion and shrugged into one of the complimentary hotel gowns.

She found Donovan in the lounge room, snarling into the phone. "I don't give a fuck," he shouted. "How did she get up here?" He was quiet for a moment. "Then take her off that fucking list. I can't even remember submitting a list." He slammed the phone down and shoved a hand through his hair.

He looked at her, his gaze intense. "What did she say to you?"

Makayla scowled. "She told me that you won't be interested in teaching me for long, that you prefer experienced submissives."

He cursed, a muscle ticking in his jaw indicating just how tense he was. "You know that she's full of shit, right? She knows nothing about what I want or what I need. If she did, we'd still be together."

"She also said that she allowed you to do anything to her and you told her she was the best sub that you'd ever had."

He barked a laugh. It was short and sharp and held no humor. "Do you know what Dolores means in Spanish?" He didn't wait for Makayla to answer. "It means pain. She hates it, of course, and prefers to go by Lola, but the funny thing is, the name fits her to a tee. She enjoys pain, both causing it and receiving it. So to a certain extent, what she said was true. She really didn't have any hard limits, but you're mistaken, angel, if you think that's what I want or even enjoyed."

He stepped toward her and grasped her around the waist. "The sort of disregard that Dolores shows for her own wellbeing and the wellbeing of others borders on psychotic. She is spiteful and venomous and I don't want her anywhere near you."

She looked up at him. "Was she the best sub that you ever had?"

"Perhaps I thought so at one point. I don't believe that any longer." Donovan tightened his hold on her. "I believe I have the best sub for me, in my arms, right now." He nuzzled her neck. "You did very well last night, baby, but I don't think paddling your ass had the effect that I was after."

She frowned. "Is that why you wouldn't let me come?

"Yes, you needed to be punished, and when I checked you, you were wet. My beautiful sub likes to have her ass paddled."

Makayla melted in his arms, his deep voice washing over her and soothing her taut nerves. "It wasn't fair," she whispered. "You left me aching."

He swept his mouth across her jaw to brush against her lips lightly. "Did you touch yourself while I slept?"

His voice was a soft purr, but she detected the undercurrent of danger. What would he do if she said that she had? A shiver of excitement rippled down her spine at the thought of him punishing her some more, but then she thought about his withholding her pleasure from her and her ardor cooled immediately. She didn't want him to do that again.

"No, Sir," she murmured against his lips.

"Did you want to?"

"Yes, it was aching."

"What was aching, baby?" He'd recommenced nuzzling her neck, sending little sizzles of pleasure directly to her nipples.

"I was aching deep in my belly," she breathed.

"Are you aching, now?"

"A little. It's starting again."

He hummed against her throat. "We'll have to do something about that."

He loosened her robe and stepped back, leaving her feeling bereft of his touch. She whimpered, but he just ignored her and focused his attention on her nipples, which were lengthening under the weight of his gaze.

"Perfect." He reached out and tweaked her nipple, sending a bolt of pleasure deep to her core. He cupped one of her breasts, testing its weight, and palmed the other mound, sweeping the flat of his hand across her erect nipple.

She moaned and arched into him. "See how swollen your breasts are?" he breathed. "When you're aroused the blood vessels dilate. It's beautiful to watch." He studied her a moment longer then bent to suck a turgid nipple into his hot mouth, swirling his tongue around the erect peak and making her groan. How could she feel that, deep inside? It always amazed her, like she was hardwired from her nipple to her clit.

He grasped her around the waist, picked her up and laid her out on the lounge. He rearranged her gown, opening it fully, and gripped one of her ankles to drape her leg over the arm of the sofa and widen her thighs.

He knelt on the floor between her legs and stared at her pussy, licking his lips before taking his index finger and running it so lightly through her folds that she barely felt his touch. He bent his head toward her and inhaled deeply. "You smell so good, angel. Like sex and pheromones."

She groaned. That unfulfilled ache from the previous night resurrected itself. She wanted to squeeze her legs together, but she couldn't, Donovan was in her way. "Please, Sir," she begged. He was deliberately drawing out her torment—she recognized it now.

"Control it, Makayla. Learn to enjoy the anticipation, let it work for you. I'm not a wham-bam-thank-you-ma'am kind of guy."

She breathed deeply and focused her energy on controlling her arousal.

Again, Donovan drew his finger so softly through her center that it was a feather touch. She thrust her hips up, unable to stop her body's automatic reach for more. Donovan slapped the side of her thigh and whipped the robe's belt from around her waist, then, picking her up, he moved her to the open end of the lounge. It never ceased to amaze her that he could carry her so easily and seemingly without effort on his part.

He positioned her on her back, bent her left leg and tied one end of the belt around that ankle, then he looped it around each of her wrists behind her back before bending her right leg and tying the other end of the belt around her right ankle. She was bound, her hands behind her back and her legs wide, wholly bared and exposed to him and unable to move. Her heart rate accelerated and delicious anticipation trickled down her spine. This was what she liked, giving total control to Donovan, passing him all the decisions so she could relish in his sex god Dom experience.

Donovan sat back and stared at her. "My baby likes being tied up," he said, his voice a low rumble. "Look at how wet you've become just in the last two minutes." He swept two fingers through her folds and circled her clit.

She groaned.

Finally, he bent his head and licked through her center. *Oh God,* that was what she'd been waiting for. He swiped his tongue up one side of her pussy lips then down the other before plunging it inside. She tried to move, tried to thrust her hips forward to get more friction, but her bound position prevented it. She was immobile and totally at Donovan's mercy.

He devoured her thoroughly, swirling his tongue through her folds and jabbing it into her before pulling back and once again licking up either side of her hole, each time avoiding her clit—it was agony and bliss, and it was driving her crazy. She bit her lip to keep from crying out her frustration and deepened her breathing. She knew he was testing her and pushing her limits by deliberately evading the one spot she needed his attention most.

He drew back and she watched him under heavy lids as he shrugged out of his dress shirt. She licked her lips, running her gaze over his chiseled chest. It was muscular perfection and tanned a golden brown from his morning swim sessions.

Donovan tossed his shirt aside and lunged forward, grasping both her butt cheeks before closing his mouth over her center and sucking, hard. A cauldron of banked pleasure suddenly bubbled to life deep in her core and she cried out. He nipped her clit then sucked it into his mouth—and that was what she needed to finally send her tumbling over the edge and into an intense orgasm. She shuddered and arched her back, wanting to close her legs but unable to. She throbbed and writhed in place, blinding white hazing her vision.

"Oh God," she mumbled drunkenly as Donovan sucked the pulses from her body.

She hardly registered when he stood and removed the rest of his clothes. Then he was before her gloriously naked, his body hard and powerful and his thick cock rearing up, veined and beautiful, to reach his navel. He fisted his shaft and pumped lazily a couple of times, a thick bead of pre-cum oozing out of his tip. She whimpered and gazed at him hungrily.

Donovan groaned and pumped his fist harder, milking more pre-cum from his tip. "You look so fucking erotic, tied up like that and at my mercy," he ground between clenched teeth. "Do you want my cock, baby?"

She nodded and bit her bottom lip anxiously.

He angled his head to one side. "I think I'll fuck your mouth. Now, with my cock in your mouth and with you bound like this, it's hard to get your safe word across. This is where you have to have the utmost trust in your Dom, and this is where I have to be careful to give you only what I think you can handle. If it does get too difficult for you, I give you permission to do what you have to, to get your point across, if you understand my meaning." He gave her a piercing look. "This is also obviously where I have to trust in my own instincts if I don't want to end up a very sore man."

He positioned himself over her, his knees on either side of her shoulders. "Open up," he ordered.

She opened her mouth wide. God, she couldn't wait to taste him. Then he pushed his hard length between her lips until he was lodged deep inside her mouth, his tip brushing the back of her throat. She relaxed her jaw, breathed through her nose and swallowed, her throat muscles contracting around his crown.

"Oh, fuck," he groaned. He stared into her eyes, his heavy lidded and hazed with lust. "You look. So. Fucking. Hot with my cock deep in your throat. Keep your eyes open."

He fisted her hair and maneuvered her head back, his gaze boring into hers. He manipulated her head forward until she was once more swallowing his length.

"That's it, baby," he groaned. "Take as much as you can."

He withdrew and plunged forward, using her hair to direct her head to where he wanted it. She opened wider and used her tongue to run along his length, swirling it around the sensitive tip.

"I'm gonna come hard and fast, baby. You're a fucking natural at this."

His breathing had increased and his jaw was tight with the tension of maintaining his control. Sweat dampened his brow and his abdominals rippled deliciously with his lunges. He pumped her mouth harder, his length swelling to impossibly large proportions.

Makayla fought back her gag reflex and kept her jaw relaxed, reveling in his masculine taste of musk and salt. Pre-cum seeped out of his tip to mix with her saliva and lubricate his glide through her lips.

His hold on her hair tightened and his movements grew choppy and erratic. She sucked harder, closing her lips around his cock to provide a firm suction and swallowing when his shaft hit the back of her throat.

Suddenly he threw his head back and growled, gripping her hair until tears formed in her eyes, then he came. He fisted the base of his cock and fed her his cum as she stared into his eyes and swallowed, licking and sucking the head until he was clean.

"Jesus Christ," he panted, using his thumb to rub the last of his cum over her lips. "You are fucking incredible at that. I can't get enough of it."

Makayla smiled, pleased that she could provide him with so much pleasure.

Donovan quickly untied the belt from around her wrists and ankles and sat back on his heels, massaging life back into her limbs. He rubbed her legs languidly, digging his thumbs in and rotating her ankles.

"Hmm, that feels good," she murmured sleepily, allowing her eyelids to slide closed.

"Have you done that before, given a guy head?" Donovan asked, his voice low and unreadable. "You seem to be very talented at it."

She snapped her eyes open and looked at him. "Would it matter?"

He shrugged. "Not really. I guess I'd like to think that you had a virgin mouth before you met me. Stupid, I know, but the thought of you doing that to another guy does my head in."

She thought for a moment, trying to formulate her answer.

Donovan's gaze hardened. "It's an easy question, angel—yes or no? Your reticence is making me wonder if you're hiding something."

"I'm not hiding anything. I fooled around a little before I met you. I wasn't living in a convent."

Donovan raised his eyebrows. "Really?" he purred. He crawled up her body and caged her arms by her sides with his, grinding his pelvis into hers. "And what exactly does fooling around entail?" He rubbed his index finger over her lips. "What fucker has been near this mouth? My mouth?"

She huffed out a breath. "It was just a guy from school. We fooled around a couple of times. Nothing serious." She rolled her eyes. "And no, he didn't have his cock near my mouth." She giggled. "Just in my hand."

He grinned and bent his head to brush his lips softly over hers. "That's all right then," he said against her mouth. "I guess I can handle that, as long as it never happens again." He ground his pelvis into hers, circling his hips deliciously and giving a little jab to her soft center. Hard again, his cock thick and throbbing, he slid it between the lips of her pussy.

"I'm going to take you now," he mumbled, slipping his tongue into her mouth at the same time as he thrust his cock high and deep into her hungry channel.

She groaned and arched her back, accepting his solid shaft and reveling in the stretch and the feeling of fullness.

Donovan slipped a hand between them and massaged her clit, pressing down with his thumb as he swept his tongue through her mouth.

"Argh," she moaned and writhed beneath him, little tingles of pleasure zapping through her nerve endings.

He dropped his other hand to her ass and used her gathering moisture to lubricate her asshole. He pushed a finger in, knuckle deep, and the increase in pressure was extraordinary.

"I can feel my cock through your pussy," he groaned into her ear, pushing a second finger into her and stretching her hole further.

She grunted as pleasure overwhelmed her and held her breath, allowing her orgasm to take hold and rip through her, pulsating her insides with throbbing convulsions.

"Makayla," Donovan roared and followed her over, shoving into her forcefully and gripping her body tightly to his.

Chapter Thirty-One

When Makayla awoke the following morning, Donovan was gone. She recalled him murmuring to her, his lips soft against her ear as he explained about an early breakfast meeting and conference call with the bank. She'd been half asleep and had just snuggled deeper into the plush sheets, grunting a reply.

Now she was getting ready to go to the spa. She'd spent an hour after breakfast doodling some new designs in the sketchpad that she'd brought with her. She'd purchased a new set of design pencils, anxious to get started on some ideas that she'd had since she'd been in Madrid, the European city having inspired in her a range of new and exciting ideas. Since her time in Madrid, she'd decided that she wanted to re-enroll in design school. The issues with her mother, she was confident, could be sorted out. Donovan and her mother were right, she couldn't spend the rest of her life worrying about what might happen to her mum. Makayla had to get on with things, had to work on her chosen career. After she'd packed her sketchpad and pencils away, she'd gone downstairs and bought a gift for Donovan that she'd seen in the jewelers' the previous day. She hoped he liked the present. He'd done so much for her and she wanted him to know that she appreciated him, and particularly appreciated what he'd done for her mother.

She tied her hair into a topknot and shrugged into a hotel gown before leaving their suite and heading down to the spa.

She exited the elevator at the second floor and gazed from the floor-to-ceiling windows into the grand foyer below. Guests milled about chatting and taking coffee and pastries at the tables scattered around the large space. Businessmen rushed through with mobiles at their ears and briefcases at their sides, and a group of elegantly clad women stopped in the middle of the foyer to hand their many shopping bags to a harried bellhop. Then Donovan stalked into her line of vision. He'd been jogging, his tanned, muscular chest bare and beaded with perspiration, his running shirt tucked into the waistband of his shorts. He must have come back to the hotel to change while she was busy at the jewelers'. As he strolled quickly through the lobby, people stopped and stared. He had that effect on women and men alike. He was a dominant and commanding presence, oozing confidence and sophistication. From her vantage point above him, Makayla could truly appreciate the powerful masculinity that was Donovan. Her heart stuttered and that light fluttering started up in her belly.

The group of women shoppers ogled him, licking their lips and narrowing their eyes in predatory intent, their eyes widening when they spotted the eagle scarred into his back. Makayla knew what they were thinking. Donovan's blatant masculinity combined with the dangerous element of his scarification had no doubt made them all wet with longing. She scowled at them, a fierce feeling of possessive jealousy twisting her insides. She understood what Donovan meant when he talked about being driven crazy by thoughts of her with someone else, even hating other men looking at her with hunger in their eyes. She sighed in resignation, turned away from the window and entered the treatment rooms behind her.

"Welcome, Miss Carrington," a young woman greeted her. "Mr. Martínez has instructed that we are to provide you with any service that you wish. Totally complimentary, of course."

Makayla faltered, taken aback by Fernando's generosity. Other than the Brazilian wax, she had no idea what the spa offered.

"I've taken the liberty of organizing a treatment package for you," the woman continued. "You'll be having your wax, but I've also scheduled you for a Turkish bath, an aromatherapy massage and a hydration facial." She smiled. "I hope this is to your liking?"

"Yes. Thank you very much."

The young woman handed her some paperwork, asked her to complete the forms and said that she would return for her in a few minutes.

Makayla settled into a soft armchair. The scents of herbal oil and sandalwood hung thick in the air, and relaxing music filtered into the room through hidden speakers. It was a calming and soothing environment and she was looking forward to spending the next few hours being pampered in her very first spa treatment.

* * * *

Donovan flung his clothes off and stepped into the shower. He didn't know where Makayla was. She hadn't mentioned anything about going anywhere, but when he'd left earlier, she had still been half asleep. She'd probably gone out for a walk or to do some shopping, or she could be at the pool.

He soaped up and washed his hair quickly, eager to finish up and find his little submissive, his angel. It was odd and he was the first to admit it, but even a few hours without her in his company made him edgy. It was a Dom trait to a certain extent, needing to keep his sub safe and wanting to know where she was, although it hadn't been Donovan's way before Makayla. His other submissives he'd been content to leave to their own devices in their own time. Makayla was different—he worried about her, he worried that Dolores would drive her away, or that Makayla would meet someone else, another Dom who would attract her attention. It was stupid and unreasonable, but he'd never felt this way about another woman and he knew that despite what she said, Makayla was still inexperienced in the ways of the world. Her sheltered life had guaranteed that. She was still an innocent in many respects and he was driven to protect her. He knew he'd have to temper his excessive concern for her safety, but at this point in time, with his ex sniffing around, Martínez showing unwarranted interest and while Donovan trained Makayla in the lifestyle, it was a precarious period and he would have to step very carefully until he had more control of the situation. He hated feeling out of control—it was a sensation so unfamiliar as to cause him physical and mental torment—and he'd do everything in his capacity to restore equilibrium and ensure that the balance of power was once more in his favor.

He stepped from the shower and rubbed his body vigorously with a towel. He picked up the cologne that he'd recently purchased with Makayla, Armani's Aqua Di Gio. It was a good scent and he wanted something different with Makayla, something new that she'd chosen for him. Scents had a way of imprinting on the mind and flooding it with both good and not so good memories, and all his subsequent memories he wanted to be of Makayla. She was lucky, in a way. He was the only man she'd ever been with. Consequently she didn't have to try to erase her more unpleasant encounters. He splashed a little of the cologne on his neck and sprayed himself with deodorant. He dressed quickly in a pair of black cargo shorts, a polo shirt and Vans. He'd start at the pool deck and if Makayla wasn't there, he'd head to the foyer.

* * * *

He'd looked everywhere. Frantic, he glanced at his watch. It had now been over three hours since he'd guessed she'd left their suite as she hadn't been there when he'd returned from his run. If she knew that she'd be gone for so long, why didn't she leave a note? She knew that he worried about her, particularly as she was in an unfamiliar city and didn't speak the language. Madrid was a fairly safe place, but not many people spoke English, so if she had gotten lost, she might have a hard time finding someone who could help her. And she hadn't taken her fucking phone — why would she leave without it? He'd picked up the hotel phone to call Fernando when he heard the elevator ping to a stop outside the suite.

He crossed his arms and leaned against the wall, affecting a casual stance when he felt anything but casual. This had better be her at the door and not one of the hotel staff.

The door clicked open and she stepped in wearing nothing but a fucking bathrobe. Where the hell had she been for three hours dressed like that? And where the fuck was her collar? Why had she taken it off? He stared at her for a minute, his gaze boring holes through her, transmitting his immense displeasure.

Then he advanced on her like a panther stalking its prey. She took a step back, flattening her spine against the door, her violet eyes wide in anxiety. Good, she should feel fucking anxious. He reached her and flattened his palms on the door either side of her head, caging her in.

He dropped his head to speak in her ear, his voice low. "Where is your collar and where the fuck have you been for over three hours dressed like that?"

"I was at the spa," she whispered. "They asked me to take my necklace off so it wouldn't get oil on it."

Of course, he hadn't even considered the spa, forgotten, in fact, that there even was one at the hotel.

"Did you not think to leave me a note?"

"I'm sorry, I wasn't expecting to be gone so long. When I got there they told me that Fernando had organized a complimentary treatment package."

Fucking Martínez strikes again, causing him grief.

"Where is your collar?" Donovan kept his voice low, his lips brushing her ear.

"In my pocket."

She fumbled around and withdrew her collar from the depths of the robe. He straightened and took it from her trembling fingers.

"Turn around, angel."

She gave him her back and he clasped the collar securely around her neck. He bent his head to speak once more at her ear. "Do not take it off." He brought his hand up to her face and caressed her cheek. "This is mine. This collar signifies that. Soon I'll lock it in place and only I will have the key."

She shivered, her body trembling against his. He leaned closer to her, grinding his hard cock into her ass. He was still angry with her, but he was also turned on. She did things to him that no other woman ever had. Her slight body trembling against his in her anxiety was so fucking hot. He knew she wasn't scared — she was apprehensive and nervous about what he was going to do, and he loved keeping her off balance.

"Go into the bedroom, get naked and kneel by the door."

Chapter Thirty-Two

Naked and kneeling by the door, Makayla bowed her head in supplication. Her heart rate hammered a wild tattoo. Donovan loved keeping her guessing and heightening her anxiety by drawing out her anticipation. She waited for what seemed liked hours, but in reality, it was probably only ten minutes. Finally, she heard him enter the room and saw his feet as he stopped in front of her. His delicious male scent of cologne and musk washed over her, heightening her desire and need for him.

He walked to the dresser in the corner and rummaged in the drawer, collecting items, but Makayla couldn't see what they were. He strode back into her line of vision, bent, and tied a black scarf around her head, blindfolding her. She felt him behind her, then his arms were around her and he lifted her up. Depositing her on her back on the bed, he gasped — the sound loud in the silence of the room.

"What the fuck? What have you done to your pussy?"

Makayla couldn't tell if he was angry. "I had a Brazilian, to surprise you," she whispered.

He ran his fingers through her smooth folds then she felt his mouth on her, his tongue licking a hot trail though her center. She moaned and pumped her hips up.

"It had better have been a woman who did this to you," he said into her pussy.

"Yes, of course." She writhed under his ministrations. "Do you like it?"

"Hmm," he hummed against her flesh.

The vibrations sent tingling shocks through her.

"I do, but I wish you had asked me first. I would have liked to have watched. I'll have to be careful here, you'll be sensitive."

He licked her gently, almost delicately, and she groaned, the feeling so good. Then suddenly he was gone and she felt him securing her wrists and ankles to the bedposts until she was bound in a star shape to the bed. Lastly, he attached clamps to her nipples.

"I've decided on your punishment." He spoke in her ear. "You'll have to be strong, baby."

Oh God, what was he going to do? Anxiety flooded her veins and her breath stuttered. She felt something rubbery and wet between her thighs then a buzzing noise started. She jumped when the thing slid over her clit and vibrations rocked through her—a vibrator. He was using a vibrator on her. She relaxed and focused on the sensations as Donovan swept the vibe over her folds, stopping on her clit for a moment then plunging the tip into her channel.

She felt the first stirrings of an orgasm. Her insides fluttered, the muscles starting to contract. Donovan removed the vibrator and pumped his fingers in and out of her, sweeping them through her channel in circles, stretching and widening her. She grunted at the pleasure-pain of the intense sensation.

"I can tell that you're close, baby," Donovan said raggedly. "I feel you starting to clench."

She held her breath, the spread of her thighs making it that little bit harder to reach what she was striving for. She was so close, her climax within her grasp, when suddenly, Donovan withdrew his fingers, leaving her bereft, and her orgasm abated as suddenly as it had started.

She whimpered, her core throbbing with the ache of dissatisfaction.

Then his mouth was on her nipple, sucking and licking before he attached a clamp to the taut peak. He did the same to her other breast.

"Open your mouth," he murmured.

She did as he had asked and he put the chain connecting the clamps between her teeth. She drew her head back and groaned as the clamps tightened and elongated her nipples.

He lay between her thighs again, working his tongue around the folds of her pussy expertly. He swept his tongue around and around, up and down either side of her clit, but always missing the little bundle of nerves. She cried out, tears of frustration seeping out of her eyes.

He sucked her clit into his mouth and inner stirrings reawakened, bringing her orgasm flaring back to life. She started to pulse, was so close to coming that she screamed when he took his mouth away. Her orgasm retreated, leaving in its wake a hollow, empty sensation.

"What are you doing?" she sobbed.

"This is called orgasm denial, baby," he murmured from between her legs. "It's the punishment I've chosen for you."

He thrust his tongue into her channel and switched the vibrator back on, sweeping it across her sensitive clit. She shuddered and moaned in distress, not sure how long she could last. She badly wanted to come. She needed that release to take the throbbing ache away.

"Please, Donovan."

He growled and slapped her thigh. "You're not going to get ahead when you don't address me properly."

"I'm sorry, Sir," she whispered. Her emotions were close to snapping point and her insides were quaking with need.

Donovan licked up her center, pressing his tongue on her clit and massaging.

Her spread, bound legs started to shake and tremble as banked pleasure once more started to build in her core.

"Please," she begged. "I need to come."

He ignored her, flicking his tongue again and again over her sensitive clit, but the pressure wasn't quite enough to send her over the edge. She was crying now, big fat tears of frustration were running off her face to dampen her hair. She felt as if she was one big nerve ending, raw and inflamed, her skin so sensitive that a simple touch seemed to scorch her.

She snapped her teeth around the chain connecting her nipple clamps and threw her head back, desperate to focus on something else. Pain shot from her nipples to mingle with the ache in her core. *Fuck*, she screamed inwardly.

Finally, Donovan stopped his ministration to her oversensitive pussy. She felt him shift from between her thighs then he removed the scarf from her head, damp now and soggy from her tears.

Donovan knelt over her, his knees on either side of her torso. His jaw hard, his face blank and unreadable. She watched as he unzipped his shorts and pulled them and his boxers down to just under his balls, his thick cock bobbing with the motion, the tip purple and swollen, pre-cum seeping from his slit.

She licked her lips, her attention on his beautiful shaft. She forgot about her discomfort for a moment. She wanted to taste it, taste him.

But it wasn't to be. He fisted the base of his cock and pumped his hand up and down, using his pre-cum to lubricate his glide. He closed his eyes and threw his head back, groaning. His movements quickened, his fist working from his tip to his base, squeezing and pumping. The head of his cock swelled bigger, made shiny and red from its stretch. He grunted loudly and stiffened as thick spurts of cum shot out of his tip to smear over Makayla's breasts. He pumped his fist, milking out every drop of semen.

She glared at him, furious that he'd given himself pleasure after he'd tortured and tormented her so thoroughly.

"You're an ass," she hissed.

He gave her an impassive look, his chest still heaving from his personal exertions. "You'll think twice before you disobey me again."

"I didn't disobey you," she screeched. "When did you say that I couldn't go to the spa?"

"I didn't, but you know that I worry about you, particularly here, in a city that you're unaccustomed to, and your thoughtlessness has had me afraid for your safety on more than one occasion. And I hate feeling afraid. It interferes with my self-control and my equilibrium. I don't do concerned well. You could have left a message for me, you could have asked the spa staff to leave a message." He frowned. "And you touched my pussy without asking me."

Her eyes widened in disbelief. "Are you serious?"

"Very," he said grimly. "Of course, I do like what you've done with it. It will heighten your pleasure and your sensitivity."

"Fat lot of good that did me today," she grumped.

He just ignored her. "And I told you, I wanted to watch."

She rolled her eyes. "You can watch next time," she conceded.

"I know. I will do exactly what I want where you're concerned."

Of that, there was no doubt. She was his to command as he pleased and it was a position that she was enjoying immensely. However, at the moment she was feeling decidedly put out with him. Her insides felt raw and achy, and the entire encounter had made her frustrated and fractious, which she understood to be the point.

Donovan leaned over her and untied the bindings at her wrists, then moved to her ankles. He massaged life back into her limbs and rotated her joints gently. Then he unclipped one of the nipple clamps. Blood rushed to the peak and she gasped at the sensation. Donovan quickly closed his mouth over her tortured nipple, licking and laving. He repeated the process with her other breast, massaging the mound as he sucked her nipple, inflaming once again the banked ashes of her desire. Oh God, she couldn't handle much more of this.

"How are you feeling?"

"How do you think?" she spat. "That was mean and uncalled for."

He narrowed his eyes, a muscle ticking in his jaw. "Careful," he warned. "Or next time I'll draw the experience out further and I won't let you come for two days."

She climbed off the bed and stomped into the bathroom to shower. Donovan followed her in, leaning against the tiled wall nonchalantly and watching as she lathered soap over herself. She ignored him, turning her back to limit the exposure of her body.

"You don't want to test me, angel. I know what you're doing."

She finished her shower and stepped out. Donovan handed her a towel. "I'll lay some clothes out on the bed for you. We're going to Infierno again tonight and this time you'll be leaving with me."

He stalked out of the bathroom and left her to finish her ablutions in peace.

Makayla sighed, she supposed that the distractions at Infierno would at least be better than glaring at Donovan all night.

Chapter Thirty-Three

Donovan held tightly to Makayla's hand as they entered Infierno.

"*El Rey*," Carlos greeted him and gave Makayla a long once-over.

Donovan's jaw tightened. Of course, Carlos was accustomed to women at Infierno being largely available, and Donovan had never had a problem sharing, provided, of course, that the woman was willing. But this was different. Makayla was different, and the sooner that these assholes understood that, the better.

"Back off, Carlos," Donovan warned, his voice dangerously low. "She's mine. I don't even like another man looking at her, understand me?"

"O, o, of course." Carlos was obviously confused as to Donovan's change in attitude. "*Lo siento, Rey,*" he apologized.

Donovan glanced down at Makayla and wondered yet again if he'd been wise in choosing such an outfit for her. She wore a tight red corset that he'd laced for her, pulling the ties as tightly as they'd go. Her breasts spilled over the top of the neckline, part of one cherry-red areola just visible. *Fuck.* He groaned inwardly — just looking at her had him as hard as nails. Her waist was made so tiny by the constriction of the corset that he could span it with both his hands — he'd tried it already back at the hotel. Her hips flared from her slim midriff and her ass, round and pert, was even more desirable because of the differential. She wore a black leather miniskirt, fishnet stockings and platform heels. She was fucking sex on legs and he'd have to watch her closely. She'd have every male in the place panting for her.

He wrapped an arm around her middle, splaying his palm across her hip possessively, and guided her through the curtain to the inside of the club.

For a moment, people stopped what they were doing and stared at them. He'd always drawn a curious crowd here — people who didn't know him wanted to, and those who did know him wanted to be seen with him. He figured that with Makayla on his arm, they made for a more interesting spectacle.

He guided her to the bar, picked her up and deposited her onto a barstool.

"Two glasses of *cava*," he ordered from the bartender.

He looked at Makayla, her face tipped up to his, her mouth parted slightly, her plump lips painted cherry red and glossed to a high shine. He dipped his head and licked them, marveling at the taste of real cherries that burst on his tongue. Fuck, this woman would be the death of him. He literally couldn't get enough of her. He closed his eyes and inhaled her scent, reveling in her.

The bartender passed across two glasses of their best *cava* and he handed one to Makayla, clinking her glass with his.

They each took a sip, Donovan eyeing her overflowing cleavage. He reached a hand up and traced the exposed part of her areola with his index finger.

"I wonder, should we leave this visible?" he mused.

Makayla looked down and blushed when she realized to what he was referring. He loved it when she reddened—her cheeks rosy with embarrassment or modesty were a huge turn-on for him. She automatically went to pull the corset up to cover it, but he stilled her movements.

"I think we'll keep it. I love that I'm the only man who can even look, let alone touch." He dipped his head again and dropped a kiss to her areola.

"You can't stop men looking at me," Makayla pointed out.

"I can and I will," he snarled. "But then again..." He looked thoughtful. "I do like that men can look at you with longing but they can't touch—they can never touch. There's a certain...selfish enjoyment in knowing that other men want what's mine."

Makayla looked at him askance. "You really are kinky, you know that?"

He chuckled. "I've never denied it, baby."

He'd decided that he would to take Makayla to one of the private rooms. They had two-way glass mirrors, so the inhabitants could see out, but no one could see in. There were also rooms that worked in the reverse. However, he wasn't about to let anyone see Makayla as she climaxed—that privilege was for him alone.

"I have to go and organize something. I'll be right back." He dropped a kiss to her head then walked toward the club manager to organize a room for them.

He returned as quickly as possible, unwilling to leave Makayla alone for too long in such an environment. Even though she was clearly collared, it wouldn't stop some men from trying something. As he reached the doorway to the bar, he realized he was right to be concerned when he caught sight of a large, burly man sitting next to Makayla. Donovan stared for a minute, trying to work out if he knew the interloper, but he didn't think he'd seen him before. He wore a black leather vest, an emblem on the back clearly indicating that he belonged to an American motorcycle club and black leathers covered his thick legs. Each of his arms sported tattoo sleeves, the designs snaking around his biceps and forearms like evil serpents. Donovan assessed him. The man was big, but Donovan guessed he'd be slow. He hoped he didn't have to test his theory. As he watched, the man moved closer to Makayla, and when he reached a hand out to caress her chest, Donovan saw red. His vision hazed over and he started shaking. *How dare the fucker touch her and touch her* here! Makayla had leaned away from him, but the bastard had just sidled closer, absolutely ignoring her bid to keep her personal space.

He stalked toward them, blood pumping furiously through his veins. He overheard the bartender warning the fucker to keep his distance, but the bastard just laughed and disregarded him. Taking it as a personal challenge, the guy positioned himself directly in front of Makayla. Donovan saw his beady eyes haze with lust as his gaze traveled her body.

He growled low in his throat, the sound so like a wild animal's that both Makayla and the biker glanced in his direction. He was on them in a second. He grasped Makayla around the waist and hauled her off her stool, pulling her tightly to his side.

"What do you think you're doing, motherfucker?" he snarled. "You just touched something that's not yours to touch!"

The other man chuckled. "Who she belong to, you?"

Donovan slipped a finger under Makayla's collar. "You're obviously not from here or you'd know that this means that she belongs to me. Now fuck off before I rearrange your ugly face."

The biker laughed, a full belly sound, and threw his head back. "I think I want to keep her for me," he said. "I like her. She's the best piece of ass that I've seen since I've been in this city."

He reached a hand toward Makayla and that was it. Donovan lost the remnants of his control. He pulled his fist back and sent it rocketing forward, connecting with the man hard in the face and sending him staggering backward. He rocked on his feet for a second, blood pouring from his nose, then rage suffused his features and he sent his own fist swinging, but Donovan was ready and ducked, the biker ending up flailing at thin air.

Donovan lifted his fists, ready to defend himself, and threw a second punch. Carlos and one of the dungeon monitors burst onto the scene. They manhandled the burly biker, twisting his arms behind his back and shoving him toward the exit.

Donovan grasped Makayla to him and kissed the crown of her head. "Are you okay, baby?"

"I'm fine, Donovan." Her voice was muffled by his shirt.

He pushed her away and held her at arm's length, examining her. "He fucking *touched* you," he seethed.

"I could have handled things by myself," she responded petulantly.

"Makayla, he was three times your size. And *you* shouldn't have to handle anything, especially not here. It's my job to look after you, particularly in an environment like this."

Donovan shook his fist and flexed his fingers. That guy had a fucking hard head.

Makayla took his hand and checked his knuckles. "Did you hurt yourself?"

"No, I'm fine," he said irritably. "I don't even know how that biker found himself here. I guess he's in Madrid for the bike exhibition and I'm assuming he had a personal invite from one of the Infierno members. Forget about it." He hooked his finger through the loop on her collar and pulled her to him. "Come, I have a surprise for you."

Makayla followed dutifully as Donovan tugged her along behind him. He opened a door, ushered her inside and unhooked his finger from her collar. Makayla looked through the large window taking up one wall of the room. Through it, the main area was clearly visible, where different scenes were being played out. Groups of people milled about observing, or were involved in their own separate play.

"Come here," Donovan murmured. He stood next to a strange-looking bench with chains and cuffs attached.

Makayla walked over hesitantly. What did he have planned?

"Remove your skirt, shoes and stockings," he ordered.

She gulped and looked back at the mirror.

"They can't see in," he assured her. "Only we can see out, which adds a certain erotic element to things."

She did as he asked and felt strangely more exposed than if she'd been completely naked. Something about having her bottom half bare while her top half was still clothed somehow seemed more indecent. He gave her a knowing smirk, which made her think that he knew exactly what she was feeling.

"Bend over the bench and put your knees on the knee pads. Grasp those handles."

Makayla positioned herself on the bench with her ass high in the air and gripped the handles at the bottom.

"That's perfect, my angel. I'm going to spank you now, but this is for your pleasure and mine. Do you understand?"

Desire flooded her veins and she shivered in anticipation. "Yes, Sir."

"Place your face to the side, so you can watch what's going on outside."

She turned her head so her cheek was flush against the cool leather of the bench. She heard Donovan moving around behind her, smelled his cologne and his unique male scent.

She heard something whip through the air, then his hand landed on her ass cheek with a loud clap. She jumped, startled, and gulped a breath as the sting radiated outward.

"Breathe deeply, baby. Absorb it," Donovan instructed.

He rained slaps down on her backside, alternating the smacks between her left and right ass cheeks with smacks between her thighs. The pain of Donovan's slaps mingled with her pleasure, leaving her raw and sensitive. The stirrings of her desire reignited and took hold deep in her core.

He landed another strike on her ass cheek, the slap sounding loud and sharp in the enclosed space.

Donovan groaned. "Your ass is such a fabulous shade of pink, baby."

His breathing came in short, sharp bursts. He swept his fingers through her folds and grunted in satisfaction. "You're so fucking wet. You love me spanking you, don't you?"

"Yes, Sir," she gasped, lightheaded with desire. She didn't think she could handle it if he denied her again. He plunged his fingers in and out of her channel, sweeping them around in large circles. She moaned and writhed and took deep breaths. The pinch of pain mixed with pleasure sent her so close to the edge that she shuddered, her limbs trembling as she strived to stop from climaxing. Donovan hadn't said that she could, and his denial of earlier made it so much more difficult to retain control.

He slapped her four more times. She groaned, her ass cheeks hot and raw to the touch, moisture dripping down her thighs. Something cool and wet touched her skin. Donovan lathered her backside with cream, sweeping his large palms across her ass cheeks and massaging the ointment into her flesh. Then he picked her up. She fell against him, limp and exhausted.

"I'm not finished with you yet, baby," he murmured in her ear, walking over to another contraption.

God, there was more? She wasn't sure how much more she could take, but seeing as she had yet to climax, she was willing to stick it out. She desperately needed the release. Her insides throbbed so badly that she was concerned she'd never feel normal again.

Donovan placed her gently on her feet and fiddled with the straps on another bench, this one looking alarmingly like a medical device.

"Get on the bench and position your legs in the stirrups."

She climbed shakily onto the bench, the leather cool under her flushed skin, and placed her legs in the leg supports either side.

Donovan strapped her wrists into cuffs above her head and her feet into the stirrups so she was positioned in a bizarre replica of a gynecological exam. Infierno's club inhabitants performing their kinky scenes were exhibited before her, visible through the window like an erotic drama performed for her pleasure alone.

Donovan stepped into her line of vision and stared at the juncture of her thighs. "I love that I can see all of your pussy. So beautiful, so wet and swollen with arousal." He groaned. "Fuck, it's the epitome of a Dom's wet dream. You strapped in with your legs spread wide, exposed to me fully."

Makayla focused her attention on the bulge at his crotch. Wanting his cock inside her mouth, inside her pussy—needing it.

Donovan stepped forward and forced her corset down so her breasts were pushed up and above the rigid boning. He bent his head and sucked one turgid nipple into his mouth, drawing on it in long, slow pulls that she felt deep in her core. He sucked a moment longer then nipped the tip, making her groan.

He straightened and stepped between her spread legs. "Look at me," he demanded.

Makayla snapped her eyes open and met his, heavy-lidded and hungry with lust. He swept his fingers along her wet folds, gently at first, then he applied more pressure, massaging her pussy lips with an almost painful rub. She was so sensitive, so taut with unrelieved tension, that the slightest touch seemed amplified tenfold.

She moaned, but kept her eyes open and on Donovan, determined to do what he wanted, desperate for the release that had been out of her grasp all day.

He thrust one finger then two inside her, pumping them slowly and methodically through her swollen pussy lips. He added a third finger and pushed high and deep.

"Just here," he murmured, rubbing the front of her channel wall and staring at her intensely.

"Oh God," she cried out, and grasped the cuffs in her fists. Her body trembled, her bindings only allowing for minimal movement, ripples of pleasure radiating from her core. He thumbed her clit, pressing on the little bundle of nerves as he massaged her G-spot. Her limbs shook and she gulped in deep breaths, trying to impede the climax that was threatening. *Fuck, when is he going to allow me to come?*

"I know you're close. You can come," he rasped, thrusting his fingers higher and deeper.

She let go and cried out a garbled version of his name as the waves of pleasure pulsed through her. Bright spots of light blinded her and her whole body quivered with the force of her orgasm, the spread of her legs seeming to prolong the pleasure.

She slumped back against the bench in exhaustion, her limbs feeling boneless and jelly-like. The throbbing ache in her core had dissipated, leaving a pleasant warmth in its place.

Suddenly there was a whirring, mechanical sound and the bench started to move upward, making her gasp in surprise.

"I can position it where I want it," Donovan explained. "And I want you level with my cock."

The bench shuddered to a stop, her spread legs now lined up with his crotch.

"That's perfect," he murmured, unzipping his pants and shoving them and his boxer briefs down to rest under his ball sac, liberating his erect cock to rest heavily against his tight abs.

It was a sensual sight, so erotic and sexual that the muscles in her sex clenched in anticipation.

"I'm going to take you now. I can't wait a moment longer to be inside you. You can come at will."

He shuffled closer, scooped his palms under her ass and thrust into her.

They groaned in unison. He pulled back and lunged forward, jamming his cock so deeply into her that she saw stars and felt him bump against her cervix.

"Fuck," she yelped in pleasure-pain.

He grunted and slapped her thigh, withdrawing for a third powerful thrust. The rigidity of the bench allowed no give, so Donovan could drive into her forcefully and relentlessly.

She sobbed and gripped the chains that bound her wrists as Donovan powered his cock into her. The feeling was unbelievable. She was stuffed full of him, totally impaled and at his mercy.

He grasped her ass with one hand and used his other to massage her clit, spreading her moisture around the nub of nerves and pressing hard.

She cried out and jerked in her fastenings, blinding pleasure streaking her vision white and scorching through her insides. Her internal muscles pulsed and quaked, milking Donovan's cock forcefully as her swollen tissues gripped him like a fist.

"Fuck, baby!" he shouted and thrust twice more, burying himself deeply and filling her with his hot cum.

Chapter Thirty-Four

Makayla lay limply on the bench, Donovan collapsed on top of her but using the armrests to support the bulk of his body. Donovan's head rested next to hers, his warm breath puffing over her face.

There was a sharp rap on the door then it opened.

Makayla jumped in surprise. Donovan raised his head and growled low in his throat, the terrifying sound startling Makayla more than the surprise entry. He adjusted his body over hers, concealing her from whoever had just entered the room unannounced.

"There had better be a very good fucking reason for interrupting my scene and bursting in on my girl while she's naked!"

Donovan stiffened in anger. She wanted to put a reassuring hand on his arm, but she was still immobilized. At any rate, her back was to the door so anyone entering would see very little of her. With a start, she realized that Donovan had referred to her as 'his girl' and not his sub, which she would have expected. Perhaps Donovan thought of her as something more, and the idea sent a warm feeling flooding through her. She loved being Donovan's sub, but she would also love being his something more.

"*Lo siento, Rey.*"

Makayla recognized the apology and Donovan's last name, but then the man continued in rapid Spanish, losing her entirely.

Donovan snapped a brief reply. When the man was gone, Donovan peeled his body away from hers then quickly he set about releasing her bindings. He picked her up and carried her over to a lounge that she hadn't noticed sitting in the corner of the room, depositing her onto the cushions and arranging a blanket over her.

"Didn't you lock the door?" she now thought to ask.

"There are no locks on the doors in here. The dungeon monitors have to have access to the rooms in case of trouble." He pointed to a number of panic buttons located around the room. "Those are also for security."

Of course, she'd never thought of that.

"I'm needed for a moment in one of the other areas." He dropped a brief kiss to the top of her head. "Are you okay here for a minute while I see to the issue?"

"I'll be fine," she assured him.

He knelt in front of her, looking troubled. "I really shouldn't leave you alone. It's imperative that I, as your Dom, provide aftercare, ensuring that you feel comfortable and safe."

She smiled. "You're not going away forever, are you?"

He returned her smile. "No, I should only be a few minutes." He straightened and left quickly, closing the door securely behind him.

Makayla stretched. The cream Donovan had used on her backside was very effective. She wasn't tender at all, but then, he'd only spanked her with his hand, and while it had stung, it hadn't been at all hard to bear. She stood and collected her clothes, which were strewn across the floor, and dressed quickly, not wanting to be caught half naked a second time. She'd just buckled the strap on her shoe and readjusted her corset when the door flew open. She looked up, expecting to see Donovan, but instead was greeted by a man that she recognized to be one of the bartenders.

"Please, *señorita*." He spoke in hesitant English. "*El Rey* would like to meet you at the front of the club. He has a car waiting."

Makayla hesitated. Why would Donovan not tell her himself? She gazed at the bartender, who shuffled from foot to foot. He looked nervous. Perhaps there had been another altercation with that biker guy from earlier and Donovan couldn't come for her personally. She wasn't concerned for her own safety. She was just worried about disobeying him, and didn't relish undergoing orgasm deprivation again any time soon.

She collected her handbag and followed the bartender. They walked briskly through the main area then the bar to the outside of the club. She thought it strange that Carlos wasn't manning his usual position at the door, but didn't dwell on it, as she was anxious to discover what had happened to make Donovan decide to leave Infierno in such a hurry.

A silver Mercedes limousine sat idling at the curb, the back door open. Makayla said a hasty goodbye to her escort then ducked into the car, the dim interior rendering it difficult for her to make anything out, and the streetlights casting barely any light inside. The driver revved the engine and took off into the Madrid traffic. Makayla squinted, trying to recognize Donovan in the dimness, but her companion didn't have the powerful physique of Donovan, nor his masculine scent. The immediate certainty that it wasn't Donovan in the car with her sent her blood cold.

"Who are you?" she asked into the dim interior, dismayed that she couldn't keep the quaver from her voice. She heard the flick of a Zippo lighter then the flame flared to life, illuminating the unmistakable features of Dolores.

Makayla gasped in shock, unable to speak for a moment. What the hell did the crazy bitch want with her? She watched silently as Dolores lit the cigarette and took a deep drag, blowing the smoke in Makayla's direction. Her lips were painted blue-black, her exotic cat's eyes outlined in inky liner, giving her a sinister appearance. Despite herself, Makayla shuddered, the full impact of her situation hitting her full force. No one knew where she was, only that bartender, but she suspected that he was in on everything that was happening to her now. And Donovan would just think that she'd run off again, as she had the last two times she'd been at Infierno.

She eyed the woman across the car. Surely she wouldn't be kidnapping her to hurt her. Why would she do that?

As if reading her thoughts, Dolores spoke, her sexy accent at odds with her spiteful demeanor. "I'm not going to hurt you, *angel*. Isn't that what the King calls you? His *angel* and his *baby*?"

Makayla remained silent, not wanting to antagonize her.

Dolores blew a cloud of smoke in the air. "You don't have to answer. I know that he does."

The interior of the car was lighter now that they'd moved into an area where the streetlights were brighter and more numerous.

"I can't quite work out what he sees in you." Dolores looked her up and down critically. "Although I suppose you have a certain innocence that appeals to him. I know him well enough to see that. It would fascinate the Dom in him." She sighed, crossing one leg over the other and resting her head back against the seat. "You know, he *is* the best Dom. Certainly the best I've ever had." She straightened and glared at Makayla. "And here he is, smitten with you." She smiled slyly. "I wonder if he's been totally honest with you, *angel*? I wonder, has he told his precious *baby* everything?"

Makayla grew tired of listening to her ramble. She frowned. "What are you talking about, Dolores, and what possessed you to kidnap me, for God's sake?"

"Don't call me that." Dolores' eyes flashed angrily. "I go by Lola or Lolita."

Makayla crossed her arms impatiently. "What. Do. You. Want?"

"Why, Makayla, I'm just trying to do the right thing by you. I'm sure, when you hear what I have to tell you, you'll be horrified. I thought it best to tell you myself, seeing as Donovan obviously has no intention of doing so."

"Tell me what?" Makayla snapped crossly. "That you're his ex-submissive or his ex-girlfriend? He already told me that."

Dolores smiled at her, a wide cat-ate-the-canary smile. "Yes," she agreed. "I am his ex-girlfriend. I stopped being his girlfriend when I became his wife."

Chapter Thirty-Five

For the fucking umpteenth time this trip, Donovan was furious. He'd gone back to the scene room to find Makayla gone, after he'd been called away to what had amounted to a wild goose chase.

He stalked to the front desk and interrogated Carlos, only to find out that he hadn't been there when Makayla left—if in fact she *had* even left the premises. It worried him that Carlos hadn't been at the desk, which meant that anyone could have wandered in. Thoughts of the biker asshole were uppermost in his mind. It was unusual that Carlos left his post at the door without having someone fill in for him, but Donovan would deal with that later.

"*Fuck,*" he roared, gripping his hair in his fists and pacing the length of the club entrance. He took a couple of deep breaths. He had to settle down and regroup.

He called Fernando at the hotel and asked him to check their suite to see if Makayla had been there. He tried her mobile number numerous times, but the fucking thing just rang.

He waited at the bar for Fernando to call him back and ordered a scotch, downing the liquor in one gulp then ordering another. He drummed his fingers on the bar impatiently then answered his mobile as soon as it buzzed.

"King, she hasn't even been here," Martínez informed him over the phone. "I've checked both the suite and the security system. Your suite's not been accessed since you two left."

Donovan thanked him. He was already on his way to the Infierno manager's office before he'd hung up. He shoved the door open, flinging it back on its hinges in his haste.

The manager shot up from his desk in surprise.

"I need to see the security footage for tonight," Donovan ordered in Spanish. "My girlfriend is missing and she was last seen here."

The manager was already at the bank of CCTV screens, rewinding the footage to after Donovan and Makayla had entered the scene room. Donovan saw himself leave the room after they'd first been disturbed. He waited with bated breath as the manager fast-forwarded the footage.

"*Paralo*," Donovan yelled when he saw a man approach the door. The manager stopped the footage and they both watched as a guy entered the room, Makayla exiting with him a couple of minutes later.

Donovan leaned toward the screen. That was the new bartender. What the fuck was he doing with Makayla? A frisson of fear worked its way down his spine. He didn't like this at all.

"Where is that motherfucker now?" Donovan snarled, his body tight with tension.

The manager looked at his watch. "*Fuera del trabajo.*"

Fuck, of course he'd be off work. "I'll need his details," Donovan snapped. "He's just about to get a wake-up call!"

* * * *

Makayla froze in shock. Dolores had to be lying. She'd wanted to cause trouble as soon as she'd seen Makayla and Donovan together.

"You're lying," she accused.

Dolores laughed, a surprisingly sweet sound for such a vicious woman. "Do you think I'd just come to you without proof? I knew you wouldn't believe me." She switched on a small overhead light. With the sudden illumination, Makayla could see the other woman fully. She wore a tight black jumpsuit and knee-high boots. The outfit and the eye makeup made her look like Batman's Catwoman, the bizarre resemblance sending Makayla into a sudden giggling fit.

The other woman glared at her. "What are you laughing about? I assure you, princess, there's nothing funny about *this*." She reached into a handbag, extracted a folder and handed it to Makayla. "What is it you English speakers say? 'Read it and weep.'"

She took the folder hesitantly. She didn't want to read what was inside. She just wanted this crazy woman to let her out of the car so she could forget she'd ever set eyes on her.

Dolores blew a smoke ring into the air and smirked at her. "Go ahead. Open it."

Makayla opened the folder with shaking hands and withdrew a sheet of paper. Although written in Spanish, she could tell it was an official document of some sort and looked suspiciously like a marriage certificate.

Dolores leaned forward and withdrew a second sheet. "This is the English version," she said, nodding at Makayla to take it from her.

She gripped the paper, knowing what she'd read on the document but wanting desperately to delay the inevitable. She looked down with blurred vision, the import taking a moment to sink in, but the meaning was undeniable. It was a marriage certificate detailing the marriage between Donovan Antonio King and Dolores María Sanchez. She scanned the document for the date.

She looked at Dolores. "This is dated over two years ago. A lot could have happened between then and now."

"Yes," the other woman conceded. "But it hasn't. We might not have" — she waved a hand in the air — "seen a lot of each other lately, but it doesn't change anything. He's *still my* husband."

Makayla shook her head, trying to regain some perspective. "You could be divorced, or legally separated for all I know. This doesn't prove anything." She held up the sheet of paper.

"If that was the case, why wouldn't Donovan have told you? Instead, he's kept it from you."

Why *would* Donovan have hidden this from her? He could have confided in her, but he had said very little about his relationship with Dolores. Had he been so vague because he had something to hide? Makayla chewed her bottom lip. She didn't know what to think.

"What do you want from me?" she finally asked.

"I want you to go back to wherever you came from. I want you out of Donovan's life."

Makayla glared at her. "Why would I do that without even speaking to Donovan about this? At the moment, I only have *your* word that this marriage is still valid."

Dolores held up a mobile phone. "Perhaps this will convince you." She swiped her finger across the screen. "It's audio only, but I'm sure you'll recognize the voices."

She heard Donovan speaking. It was a little distorted but totally recognizable.

"Why did you visit my parents?"

Then Dolores' voice. *"I was telling them about us."*

"They know about us?"

"I wanted to show them a picture of Donny. You know they love him."

"Yes. They do love Donny." Donovan's voice turned hard. *"But you have to stop this."*

"What? Stop them from seeing their grandson? Stop them knowing about us?"

"Yes. Exactly that!"

Makayla had heard enough. "Please, stop it."

Dolores dropped her mobile with a satisfied smile. "That is why you need to leave, *angel*. We have a child together—a family." She gave Makayla a condescending look. "*You* are just a diversion for him. He'll never leave me. I am his wife and the mother of his child, even his parents acknowledge that."

Makayla stared at the woman sitting across from her. The evidence did seem irrefutable. "Who is Donny?" she asked.

Dolores grinned, this time with no malice. She handed Makayla a photo of a little brown-haired boy. Makayla studied it. The boy did look a little like Donovan, and had similar features. She looked closer and saw the resemblance around the mouth and nose.

She was sure this boy was related to Donovan. In fact, everything that Dolores had produced was pointing straight to the fact that Donovan was a grade-A asshole.

Nausea swept through her. What had she done? She'd had an affair with a married man. A married man with a child, no less. She had to do what this bitch asked of her. She needed to leave. "Stop the car!"

Dolores arched an eyebrow and tapped the privacy window. "Where are you going?"

The driver slowed to a stop.

Makayla looked at her incredulously. "I want to go back to the hotel. I require my passport and personal effects. I can't leave without them."

"There's no need," Dolores informed her tersely. "I had someone retrieve your passport from Donovan's suite. I have everything here." She passed Makayla a travel wallet. "I'm going to take you to an airport hotel, so you can leave first thing tomorrow. Everything's been arranged."

"This is crazy," Makayla spat. "You should be locked up!"

Dolores gave her a hard look. "Do you really want to go back to him now? Now that you know that he's lied to you? You've been sleeping with a married man. Are you that immoral that it doesn't concern you?"

She was right. If Makayla went back to the hotel, Donovan would find her and no doubt try to talk her into staying. She knew she wouldn't be able to resist him if he did that. No, she had no choice but to go along with the bitch. Makayla had never had so many vicious thoughts about a person. This woman was really doing her head in.

"Fine," she conceded. "Take me to this hotel. You've obviously made a booking for me."

Dolores smiled. "I have. I expected you to do the right thing eventually, and you know as well as I that Donovan won't let you go without a fight. He's a Dom, and used to getting his way. Women don't leave Donovan. Only he decides when a relationship has to end." She shrugged. "But with you out of the country, he'll soon see the error of his ways."

Makayla sat back in her seat and stared out of the window. She was going home, and she'd never see Donovan again. The thought tightened her chest painfully. She loved him, she realized. Why did she have to go and fall in love with him? He was obviously a lying scumbag, a cheating, lying scumbag. But she wouldn't think about him now, she had to focus on the immediate future. She'd concentrate on getting home. She'd pick up her mother from the treatment facility, then she'd go about mending her broken heart and forgetting about the fact that she'd ever met Donovan King.

Chapter Thirty Six

Donovan bashed his fist on the bartender's door. After about fifteen minutes of banging, the fuckwit finally opened it. Donovan stepped over the threshold, shoving the guy hard.

"Where the fuck is Makayla?" he snarled.

The guy rubbed his eyes, looking confused. "What are you talking about?"

"I'm talking about the woman you left Infierno with." Donovan poked him in the chest, emphasizing each word. "Where. Is. She?"

Realization dawned on his face. "You must be the King."

"Yes. And you just fucked with my girlfriend. Kiss your job goodbye, asshole."

"I'm sorry. I didn't know who she was. Some woman paid me one hundred euros to tell her that Donovan was waiting for her in a car out front."

"Where did they go?"

"That's all I know."

Donovan glared at him a moment longer, but he thought that the jerk was telling the truth. This whole thing smacked of Dolores' work.

He stormed out of the apartment, his mind working furiously. Where the fuck could they be? He stood on the pavement and shoved his hands through his hair in frustration. His mobile buzzed. "Makayla!"

"No, it's Fernando. Have you found her yet?"

"Not yet. I think she's with Dolores."

"I just thought of something. Remember when you arrived, you asked me about a GPS tracking app for mobile phones?"

Donovan's eyes widened with the realization. He hailed the next cab.

Fernando kept talking. "Did you end up downloading it?"

"Yes. You're a genius, Martínez. I'm coming back to the hotel. I need to borrow your car."

Donovan hung up. How could he have forgotten that he had that tracking app? He'd been worried that Makayla would get lost and he'd downloaded the application so he could assist her if necessary. He pulled up the GPS tracker and waited for it to update. According to the application, she was somewhere near the airport. Fuck, he hoped she wasn't *at* the actual airport. He prayed to God that he'd get to her in time.

* * * *

Makayla got out of the car. She felt as if she were in a parallel universe, and she couldn't believe that only an hour previously she'd been at Infierno with Donovan.

Dolores leaned out of the window. "Have a safe flight," she said in parting.

She had to hold it together at least until she reached Sydney. When she got home, she had all the time in the world to cry. She didn't have any luggage. It hadn't been lost on Makayla that Dolores had retrieved her passport, but obviously hadn't been bothered with any of her personal things. She'd really wanted to make Makayla feel as uncomfortable as possible.

She decided not to think too deeply about how Dolores had managed to get access to their suite. After all, she'd gained access once before, so she probably hadn't found it too difficult. Perhaps they hadn't gotten around to taking her off Donovan's list of visitors. She looked down at what she was wearing. She couldn't get on an aircraft wearing this get-up. She'd just been at a BDSM club, for God's sake. She strode into the lobby of the hotel and nearly died of relief when she caught sight of a boutique. She walked straight over to it, surprised that it was still open, and chose a pair of shorts, a blouse with 'I Love Madrid' embroidered on the pocket and a pair of heeled sandals. She also bought some basic toiletries and a small carry-on bag. She changed in the changing room and instantly felt more at ease.

She checked in and found her room, suddenly feeling exhausted, which was hardly surprising since it was two in the morning. She wanted nothing more than a shower then to slip between cool sheets. Tomorrow, she'd think about her situation. She was undecided about contacting Donovan before she left. He was probably going absolutely crazy wondering where she was, but then again, after what she'd learned about him that evening, he really had no right to be worrying about her.

Makayla stepped into the shower and thought back to the conversation that Dolores had recorded, and replayed it in her mind. While Donovan hadn't directly said anything about their relationship, he also hadn't denied Dolores' leading statements. If they were no longer together, why hadn't he confirmed it? Instead, he'd just complained about her seeing his parents. That alone was enough to tell her that there was something more between them than Donovan had led her to believe. And there was the little boy, Donny, who looked so much like Donovan, and when Dolores had called Donovan's parents his grandparents, he hadn't denied it. Why would he need to keep his son a secret? There was only one explanation, and it was that Dolores was telling the truth.

She stepped out of the shower and wrapped herself in a hotel bathrobe. She pulled the covers back on the bed and slipped between the sheets. She was so exhausted she didn't even have the energy to cry. A numbness had taken her over, leaving her feeling disconnected from her body, as if the events of the last few hours had happened to someone else. She supposed it was better than being bombarded by all the raw emotions that she knew would come eventually. At least she could harden herself at the moment, go through the motions of getting on the aircraft and make it back home safely and as quickly as possible.

* * * *

Donovan drove like a madman to the airport. He'd quickly checked all the flights to Sydney via Dubai and there were none leaving until tomorrow afternoon. Therefore, he assumed that Makayla would be at one of the airport hotels nearby. He checked the GPS tracker. Her position hadn't moved. He headed toward the airport. There were two hotels near her position and he guessed she was in one of them. He arrived at the first one, pulled the car into the parking lot and raced inside to the reception desk.

He spoke in Spanish to the woman behind the counter. Initially, she wasn't going to confirm that Makayla was staying at the hotel, but he persevered. After calling Fernando and getting him to speak to the manager of the hotel, he eventually had Makayla's room number.

* * * *

Makayla awoke with a start. *What was that?* She listened for a moment, then it came again—loud banging on her door.

"Makayla? Open up. Now!"

It was Donovan and he sounded angry, but there was also something else in his voice, something that sounded like desperation. She chewed her lip for a moment, indecision waging a war within her. But when he started banging on the door once more, she scurried out of bed. He was going to wake the entire hotel if he kept that up.

She walked to the door and opened it. Donovan leaned against the doorjamb, his hair mussed, like he'd been running his hands through it. He looked up at her, his eyes burning with a fierce intensity.

"What the fuck, Makayla?" His voice broke. He stepped into the room and wrapped his arms around her.

She was so startled that she didn't have time to react. She just stood and let him hold her.

"I thought I'd fucking lost you," he mumbled into her hair, squeezing her tightly.

She wriggled out of his embrace and took a few steps backward, hardening her heart to him. "What do you want, Donovan?"

He gave her an incredulous look. "What do you think I want? I want to know why you left me."

She walked to the bed and sat on the edge, needing a few moments to formulate what she wanted to say.

"I spoke to Dolores," she said finally. "She told me about you two."

Donovan's face turned hard. "Pray tell, what did the bitch have to say?"

"She showed me a marriage certificate. You didn't tell me that you were married! Why would you keep that from me? It could only be because you wanted to keep your relationship a secret. You knew I wouldn't have anything to do with you if I found out."

He sighed heavily. "I'm not married to her anymore."

"But you were?"

"Briefly. I had the marriage annulled."

"And what about your son, Donny? You didn't tell me about him, either."

"I don't have a son. She's lying to you."

Makayla couldn't believe it. She'd heard with her own ears the recording where they spoke about him. Plus he bore a resemblance to Donovan.

"Please, baby. Let me explain," Donovan implored her.

He deserved that opportunity at least. She nodded and drew her hotel robe tighter around her.

He sat on the bed next to her and grasped one of her hands in his. "Donny is the son of my first cousin, Renaldo. My aunt and uncle—Renaldo's parents, were killed in a car accident when he was young and my parents became his legal guardians, so they think of him as a son. About two years ago, I was in a relationship with Dolores. She showed me what she wanted me to see in regards to her personality. She wanted me and she set out to get me, ruthlessly. She told me she was pregnant with my child. I didn't believe it because we'd never had unprotected sex, but I know that accidents happen. Her parents were friends of my parents. Our fathers are business associates, which made the whole thing all the more awkward. I married her in a brief ceremony. It was a hopeless union from the start. I didn't love her, and I was beginning to hate the sight of her. I even lost interest in dominating her. Initially, she was my sub, but after we were married, she showed her true colors. She was manipulative, vicious and insanely jealous."

From what Makayla had seen of the woman, those adjectives definitely suited her down to the ground. "How did you find out Donny wasn't yours?"

"I had a hunch. I knew that she'd be capable of anything to get what she wanted, and I needed to be sure. I'd already looked into annulment proceedings. I just needed the proof that the child wasn't mine. Of course, I was ready to help her financially. I wasn't about to let an innocent baby come to harm. When Donny was born, I had a paternity test conducted and it proved that he wasn't mine. I started annulment proceedings immediately. In Spain, there are a few instances that justify an annulment. One is mental incapacity. I knew that she was mentally unstable, but proving it would be difficult and time-consuming.

Another was that one person in the union had a child without the knowledge of the other. While this wasn't entirely true, I had a very good lawyer and we argued that what Dolores had done should constitute grounds for annulment. I wanted to avoid divorce. Divorce complicates matters and would undoubtedly include some form of spousal support, which she didn't need or deserve. I wanted to wipe my hands of her entirely and I wanted nothing connecting us."

"How did you find out that Donny was actually Renaldo's?"

"When it emerged that he wasn't mine, even though the resemblance was there, Renaldo admitted that he'd gotten drunk one night with Dolores and they'd slept together. It was obviously her plan from the beginning to trap me, and she knew that I'd refuse to sleep with her without protection. Even then, I didn't fully trust her. Renaldo and I bear a strong resemblance — our mothers were twin sisters — so she did the next best thing in her mind."

Makayla couldn't fathom the depths the woman had gone to. It was astonishing. "She played me a recording of you and her talking. She told you she'd seen your parents and Donny had seen his grandparents. From the recording, it definitely seemed that you two were still together."

"She would have recorded that when she saw me the other night. She had been to see my parents the last time they were in Spain. Donny calls them his grandparents, and Dolores is always trying to lead them to believe that there is something more between us, even though I haven't set eyes on her in a year. She was obsessed with me. I just hadn't realized that she still felt so strongly." He gave her a searching look. "Fuck, Makayla, I thought I'd lost you."

"You very nearly did," she agreed. "At first, I didn't believe her, but the photo of Donny and the recording had me convinced, particularly as you hadn't mentioned anything to me. I thought the only reason you were hiding your relationship was because everything she told me was true."

He stood and pulled her tightly to his body. "I didn't mention it because it was over and done with and I prefer not to dwell on it." He looked around the hotel room, a vague look of distaste crossing his features. "Let's go back to our hotel. While this seems pleasant enough, it's not what I'm used to."

Makayla was happy with that. She wanted to be far away from everything that reminded her of Dolores and the previous few hours. She changed quickly into the outfit that she'd just purchased, grabbed her handbag and the small carry-on that she'd bought. Donovan raised his eyebrows. "You're a light traveler."

"Yes. The only thing that Dolores bothered to get from the hotel was my passport."

Donovan swore softly. "I'll get to the bottom of that. I have no fucking idea how she managed to get into our suite."

They left the room quickly and headed down to the lobby. It was then that Makayla wondered how he had known where she'd gone. "How did you find me?" she asked curiously.

"The GPS tracker that I downloaded onto our phones when we first arrived."

They stepped into the lift and she looked up to find Donovan giving her a hard stare. "Where is your collar?"

"It's in my bag."

"What did I say about not taking it off?"

"You couldn't expect me to keep it on after what happened. I thought you'd been lying to me and that I'd been having an affair with a married man!"

They arrived in the lobby and Donovan took her hand, tugging her out of the elevator and over to reception. "She's checking out," he told the woman at the desk, handing over her key then continuing to the front doors.

Makayla struggled to keep up with him. "Donovan, don't I need to pay something?"

"No," he said tersely. "Dolores pre-paid. She didn't want anything keeping you around longer than necessary." He shook his head incredulously "That woman will obviously stop at nothing." He guided Makayla to a black BMW. "Get in."

She hopped into the passenger seat and he leaned over her to secure her seatbelt.

"I think I'm capable of belting myself in," she said petulantly, batting his hands away.

"I know, but I want to do it." He glared at her. "Don't test me anymore, Makayla."

He jumped into the driver's seat and took off out of the parking lot, winding in and out of the early morning traffic. It didn't take them long to get to the hotel, the traffic flow was good so early in the morning, and quite quickly Donovan was parking the car in the manager's spot at the Totally Five Star. He came around to her side and opened the door for her, pulling her out swiftly.

"What's the hurry?" she gasped as she was dragged up and out of her seat.

"I want you back in our suite." He looked her up and down a little disdainfully. "And out of those God-awful tourist clothes — I Love Madrid?"

"It was the only decent shirt they had," she retorted. "I could hardly get on a plane in the clothes I was wearing."

He looked at her aghast. "I should fucking hope not. You can only wear outfits like that when I'm with you. That was the other reason I was frantic. I knew how you were dressed and I had no fucking idea where you were or who you were with. For fuck's sake, anything could have happened to you."

Donovan threw the car keys to a bellhop as they passed. They reached the elevator bank and Donovan punched in their code.

"It wasn't entirely my fault," she said irritably as they stepped into the lift. "Dolores tricked me. She sent someone to tell me that you were waiting for me out front of the club."

"I know. I tracked down the asshole who did her dirty work."

"What did you do to him?"

"Nothing much. It seems that he didn't know what he was doing. Essentially, he was on an errand that she'd paid him for. "

"Well, at least you didn't punch his lights out."

Donovan laughed. "Punch his lights out? Honestly, angel, where do you get this stuff?"

"Well, you do seem to be a little hotheaded at times."

He turned suddenly and pushed her against the wall, then he grasped her arms, pushing them above her head, his face pressed to hers. "I am hotheaded, baby, when it comes to you. Don't fucking forget it."

Makayla's heart missed a beat. He was just so unbelievably hot. He took her breath away. "I'm sorry," she whispered, apologizing for running from him a third time.

The elevator pinged to a stop, and Donovan grasped her hand, tugging her out. "You will be sorry," he murmured, swiping the card through the door lock of their suite. "Go inside and get naked."

She scurried through the door and into the bedroom. She undressed hurriedly, the import of her situation suddenly hitting her. Donovan hadn't lied to her, and he wasn't a married man. Pure elation swept through her. The numbness of the previous couple of hours was gone, and she suddenly felt alive and vibrant. The feeling of bitter betrayal that she'd buried, for fear of breaking down in a trembling heap, was no longer there. And she could finally embrace the fact that she loved him. She was hopelessly enamored with him, and that comprehension both elated and terrified her.

She knelt by the door and waited for him, her heart beating erratically in anticipation. He entered soon after her and she knew that he couldn't draw out the suspense, as he usually liked to do. He was just as anxious as she.

He moved behind her, then he knelt, lifting her hair and placing her collar around her neck. The cool metal felt comforting against her skin, and she realized that she'd missed it in the short time that it hadn't been there.

Donovan's mouth was at her ear, his breath warm against her skin. "I know that this will be the last time that you take this off, baby, because I'm locking it into place now. Do you object?"

"No, Sir." Her breath hitched in eagerness and moisture gathered between her thighs. She heard a click, then Donovan showed her a small key. "I'm the only one who can remove this. Do you understand?"

She nodded. "Yes, Sir."

He gathered her hair in his hands and swept it to one side. She felt his mouth on her neck. He nibbled her skin and pressed open-mouthed kisses to her throat. "I own you," he mumbled against her flesh. "Do you understand?"

"Yes, Sir," she gasped. Her insides burned and she was hot and trembling, his mere touch scorching her.

"And I am yours," he continued. "You own me, Makayla. I can't be without you. I love you."

Makayla shuddered with jubilation, her heart soaring. He loved her! She was all sensation—every touch of his searing her to the bone. And his words, his words were affecting her more than anything else ever had.

"Yes. Please, Sir," she begged.

He hovered behind her, not touching, just close enough for her to feel the heat of his body. "Please," she implored again. She needed him to take her, was desperate for it.

He cupped her nape and urged her to lean down, his palm firm on her neck. She obeyed, bending forward until her elbows were on the floor and her ass in the air.

"That's it, baby," Donovan rasped, his voice tight with need. "I can see how wet you are. Fuck, that smooth, pink pussy is glistening for me."

He palmed her backside, sweeping his large hands over her ass cheeks then squeezing.

Her breath hitched as he massaged the fleshy mounds, spreading them apart so she felt the cool air waft across her pussy.

She heard him unzip his pants, then he thrust inside her in one hard plunge, jerking her forward so she had to claw the carpet to keep from toppling over. He drew back and lunged again, driving into her deeply and gripping her ass cheeks, spreading them wide.

"Fuck," he panted. "You're so tight."

He stretched her with his thick cock. She felt so full of him that she didn't know where he stopped and she began.

"You're mine, Makayla," he rasped and jerked forward again, burying himself deeply. "Say it."

"I'm yours," she cried, delirious with the sensations swamping her. "I'll always be yours!"

"That's right," he agreed on another fierce drive. He pulled out then lunged again. "Because you're not only my submissive, you'll soon be my wife!"

What? Had she just heard him correctly?

He bent over her, pressing his chest against her back and speaking low in her ear as he seated himself balls deep. "It's not a romantic proposal, baby, but it's the only way I want to make it—while I'm inside your tight pussy, fucking your brains out."

He reached around to her front and slid his fingers against her clit, rubbing her moisture around the nub of nerves and massaging.

She jerked beneath him as sharp tingles of pleasure radiated throughout her core.

"What do you say, Makayla?" he demanded.

He gyrated his pelvis, circling his cock inside her channel and flicking her clit, sending her spiraling into an intense orgasm, her inner muscles clenching and milking his shaft.

"Argh!" she cried out. "Yes, yes. I'll marry you!"

Donovan growled triumphantly and picked up his rhythm, slamming into her twice more before roaring her name and coming inside her in hot, thick bursts.

She lay limply under him, dazed and elated. He had literally just fucked a yes out of her. But she didn't care, she couldn't think of a better proposal. She loved him, and he'd just proved that he loved her. She would be his—forever.

About the Author

Jasmine's alter ego lives in Sydney, Australia with her husband and their Border Collie. She enjoys cooking, traveling with her husband, outdoor activities and skiing. She loves reading all genres but in particular she enjoys romance novels and thrillers and her Kindle is never far from her side.

Jasmine loves writing and is always looking for new ideas for stories that will provoke inner passions, stimulate the senses and ignite the imagination.

Jasmine loves to hear from readers. You can find her contact information, website and author biography at http://www.totallybound.com.

Totally Bound Publishing